SHOOT THE MOON
(AND MORE)

MAX ALLAN COLLINS

WOLFPACK
PUBLISHING
— EST 2013 —

WOLFPACK
PUBLISHING
— EST 2013 —

Shoot The Moon (and more)

Paperback Edition
Copyright © 2021 (As Revised) Max Allan Collins

Wolfpack Publishing
6032 Wheat Penny Avenue
Las Vegas, NV 89122

wolfpackpublishing.com

Paperback ISBN 978-1-64734-248-7
eBook ISBN 978-1-64734-249-4

SHOOT THE MOON
(AND MORE)

For David Gilfoyle –
the real Wheaty,
with apologies.

Contents

An Introduction

Shoot the Moon (my alternate title was *Wynning Streak*), was written in the first phase of my career. When I wrote the novel, I had already sold *Bait Money*, *No Cure for Death*, *Quarry*, *Blood Money*, and *The Baby Blue Rip-off*.

Between contracts, I decided to try something different. I was very much in the sway of Donald E. Westlake at the time, and my first novel (*Bait Money*, and its sequels as well) might be fairly termed "Richard Stark" pastiches. Before I knew that Westlake and Stark were the same writer, they were my two favorite contemporary crime fiction writers – indeed, they were the last two crime fiction writers to influence me in any major way. Their works sat on the same shelf, with a bookend separating them. When I learned Westlake was Stark, I simply removed the bookend. (Don loved that story.)

On its most basic level, *Shoot the Moon* was an attempt to do the kind of comic crime caper Don was known for, under his own name. He was mentoring me at the time, and I now wonder if he was irritated that I had chosen to imitate him yet again, in another fashion. When he read *Shoot the Moon*, he was not enthusiastic, and suggested I had gone overboard with the discursive approach. The version in this collection reflects a cutting and revision based on Don's generous notes (the original doesn't seem to exist).

Incidentally, the book was written in 1974 at the tail-end (sorry) of the streaking fad. The direct inspiration was a streaking incident at my cousin's wedding.

Strange as it may seem, I'd pretty much forgotten about the novel until I was sent some materials from the files of my former agent, Knox Burger, upon his passing in 2010. Knox represented me till around 1982, when he had a lackluster response to my novel *True Detective*, and I – frankly – fired him. Since that time I've been with agent Dominick Abel, who believed in that novel, which went on to win the Private Eye Writers of America "Shamus" for Best Hardcover Novel of 1983.

True Detective wasn't the first book of mine that Knox rejected – *Shoot the Moon* was. I didn't even know agents could reject a client's manuscript, but there it was. That was when I sent the book to Don Westlake, who gave me his typically helpful notes.

The revision went to Burger (and I have a hunch Don called Knox and rattled his cage for me), who finally consented to handle the thing.

As I indicated, the manuscript of "the thing" was returned to me, with a few other odds and ends, in 2010. It did not appear to have been sent out any-where, and I never received a report from Knox on any history of rejections (much less acceptance). But my career had heated up about then, with more Nolans, Mallorys and Quarrys to write, and *Shoot the Moon* became a low priority that was soon to become a faded memory.

Reading it now, many decades later, I'm not ashamed of it. It's clearly my work and rather fun. What's most surprising to me is that I see myself doing James M. Cain in it more than Donald E. Westlake. Cain was a huge influence on my first-person style and, despite the lack of cuckold-ed husbands getting bumped off in the book, the approach is very much his.

As sort of bonus features, this volume collects two short stories of mine, from the early years of my career.

The two stories were written in a writing class at Muscatine (Iowa) Community College, though I'm not sure exactly when – some time in the 1966 - '68 period. Neither story was submitted anywhere, as there really wasn't much of a market then for hard-boiled fiction. I had started sending novels out in the mail as early as the ninth grade, and wasn't shy about collecting rejection slips. But these stories just didn't seem to have a logical home. They were part of my self-schooling in the craft of hardboiled crime fiction-writing, and they were discussed in class, and went into a drawer.

They emerged in the mid-'80s when mystery writer Wayne Dundee began *Hardboiled*, a prozine that was still in existence the last time I looked, albeit not under Wayne's stewardship. Wayne, a fellow Midwestern-er, was (and is) a friend whose work I admired. He wondered if I would write something for his new magazine. Not surprisingly, I didn't have time, due to various deadlines, but said I'd be willing to show him two early stories of mine that might be publish-able. He published them both, with "Public Servant" appearing in *Hardboiled*'s first issue (Lawrence Block later re-published it in *Opening Shots*, 2000). Even-tually Wayne also serialized the first Nolan novel, *Mourn the Living*, before its various book publications (it will be gathered with *Spree* as *Mad Money* by Hard Case Crime in a year or so), written in 1968 around the same time as the two short stories here.

"Public Servant" is quite shamelessly a Jim Thompson pastiche. What is perhaps most interesting about it is that I was imitating Thompson when he was largely unknown in the mystery field. Anthony Boucher had praised him, and R.V. Cassill's famous essay celebrating *The Killer Inside Me* in *Tough Guy Writers of the Thirties* would appear in 1968, though I'm fairly sure I wrote "Public Servant" in '66 or '67.

I read Thompson in high school. I have a vivid memory of reading *Pop. 1280* (1964) in study hall. That book is very much the inspiration for my story, but I repaid Thompson putting together (with Ed Gorman) the first monograph on him, *Jim Thompson: The Killers Inside Him* (Fedora Press, 1983), which brought "This World and Then The Fireworks" into print for the first time.

"The Love Rack" is a longer story, generously described as a novella. It was an attempt to combine what I'd learned from two of my favorite writers – Mickey Spillane and James M. Cain – into one tale. The title, as any Cain buff already knows, is a reference to the Vincent Lawrence definition of a certain kind of sex-driven story situation that was his gift to Cain. That it's heavily Spillane-influenced is amusing, considering what Mickey once told me about why he didn't care for Cain: "I don't like stories written in jail cells."

I present these stories to you because the young writer I once was very desperately wanted to see his work published, and read, and I owe him that much. I hope more casual readers will find these tales lightly entertaining, and my more dedicated fans will view them as interesting, even instructive road signs on the path I would be taking.

Max Allan Collins

Shoot the Moon

Of course it's crazy on the face of it that I would run naked across the lobby of the Holiday Inn in DeKalb, Illinois, in the middle of June, after streaking had hit its peak and gone the way of swallowing goldfish and cramming into phone booths.

Crazier still when you consider that I am a short-haired, painfully straight young man, who at the time was taking summer school at Northern Illinois University to get a diploma to go with the empty folder I'd been handed at graduation a few weeks before, and had no intention of taking off my clothes in public (or robbing a bank, either) or anything else except getting that damn degree so I could maybe *work* at a bank or Holiday Inn. I'm no rebel. I'm no criminal. My father is a Methodist minister, for Christ sake!

It started one night, in mid-June, around eleven.

I was sitting beside my friend Wheaty in a booth in Sambo's, the chain pancake house across from the DeKalb Holiday Inn. Both of us were, each in his own way, trying to reason with Peter "The Shaker" Saltz, a massive guy who was All-Conference tackle and to whom we owed a total of $78 in poker losses, $48 of it mine, $30 of it Wheaty's.

Neither of us had summer jobs, as we were busy enough just going to school making up courses we'd flunked. Neither of us had anybody around to borrow money from, as most of our friends were as poor as we were, and anyway were mostly not around, having either graduated or split for the summer. Neither of us had rich parents. Neither of us had $48, or $30, or any part of the $78.

"Awk," Wheaty said.

Wheaty is a six-foot-four, gangly guy who looks like an oversize, friendly, slightly goofy rabbit. His hair is wheat-color and won't lay down. Shaker had just told Wheat he was going to do bad things to us if we didn't pay up. He was not specific, but Wheat has a good imagination. So do I.

"I tell you what," the Shaker was saying, beady little black eyes glowing under Neanderthal forehead, fringe of prematurely thinning black hair emphasizing the slope. "Since I don't want you guys feelin' like I'm stickin' it to you, I'm gonna be fair. Give me Wheat's car and we'll call it even."

"My car!" Wheat gleeped. His big hands started moving in the air, and it was like he was trying to bat mosquitoes, tread water and wave goodbye all at the same time. "Shaker, anything but the car, Shaker, that's my mom's car, it's not even mine, she's just letting me use it, I can't give it to you, Shaker, my mom would kill me."

"Maybe," I said, striving for a reasonable, calm tone, "maybe we could find some other way to pay you back. Some way besides money or Wheat's mom's car, I mean. Work the debt off, somehow."

Shaker shrugged. "I said I was gonna be fair, Kitchenette. What you got in mind?" ("Kitchenette," by the way, is indicative of Shaker's sense of humor: my name is Fred Kitchen.)

"Oh, well," I said, "there's all sorts of ways we could work it off for you."

"Name one."

"Uh . . ."

"Well?"

"There's, uh, so many ways I can't narrow it down to just one."

"Keep tryin', Kitchenette, and when you do come up with a way, make sure it's something you can do for me before I climb on that bus tomorrow morning."

Shaker, you see, didn't need the $78 we owed him. He was leaving tomorrow, going to Toronto, having been signed to a Canadian pro football team who'd given him a healthy cash bonus. So the $78 was just something he could use as an excuse to gloat.

The past several years, we had taken Shaker's money in small stakes poker games, and Shaker, having been coached over the years that "It's not how you play the game, it's whether you win or lose," resented that. He felt we had continually humiliated him. But recently, he'd had a winning streak, and we now owed *him*. It was his turn, in other words, to humiliate us.

And then, Selma had a suggestion. Did I mention Shaker's girl friend, Selma? Blond hair, blue eyes, bosomy, cheerleader Selma?

Selma suggested, "How about a streak?"

Everybody looked at Selma and said, "Huh?" or the equivalent, and Selma batted her thick, fake lashes and said, "They're having a wedding reception across the street. At the Holiday Inn. See? The guests are all standing around in the lobby and stuff."

She pointed out the window, and we looked over, and yes, we could indeed see guests milling around in the Holiday Inn lobby, dressed to the teeth.

"Wouldn't it be just *gross* if Wheaty and Kitch streaked all those wedding guests and everybody?" And Selma, having made her suggestion, began to giggle. Apparently the thought of anything gross tickled her. She and the Shaker were engaged.

"I'll do it, I'll do it," Wheaty said, with characteristic restraint. "Anything's better than paying thirty bucks, especially when you don't have it, YES I'll do it, OF COURSE I'll do it."

Everyone in the place was looking at us now, and we waited till they stopped before resuming our talk. Shaker was eating a couple dozen pancakes, and Selma was eating a hot fudge sundae. Wheat and I were having water.

The Shaker still wasn't convinced seeing Wheaty and me nude would be worth $78. But Selma was, and so Shaker said, "Both of you or no deal."

Wheaty turned to me. "Kitch? Come on. You undress all the time. There's nothing to it. Come on. Think of my mom."

I resisted that thought and said, slowly, with deliberation, "I will not take off my clothes in front of people."

Wheat was crestfallen. He already had his short-sleeve sweatshirt pulled half-way off and couldn't believe my refusal. "You won't have to take your clothes off in front of people, Kitch! Your clothes'll already be off when we run in there!"

"What's the matter, Kitchenette?" Shaker asked, with overacted mock innocence. "Got somethin' to hide?"

Selma said, "Oh Shaker, you're so *gross*," and snuggled into his behind of a shoulder.

Meanwhile, I was blushing. I admit it.

"Come on, Kitch," Wheat said. "Let's show the Shaker what we're made of."

"Shaker and everybody else, you mean," I said.

"Hell," Shaker said. "I'd rather have the seventy-eight bucks."

"Okay," I said. "Okay. I'll do it."

Don't ever try to undress in a Volkswagen.

A guy Wheaty's size has trouble getting inside a

Volkswagen, let alone stripping in one. And it goes without saying anybody Wheaty's size has no business driving a Volkswagen, if for no other reason that his knees would block his path of vision.

Wheaty drove a Volkswagen. A copper-color bug that was (as Wheat had told Shaker) still in his mom's name, even though Wheat had been driving it since high school. Riding in Wheat's bug is always an adventure in itself and perhaps all the times I'd come close to death in that rider's seat made it possible for me to withstand the dangers of streaking and bank robbery.

First, streaking.

Wheat got his elbows in my eyes and got himself caught in his fly and there was some discreet screaming from both of us, but somehow, don't ask me exactly how, we were both naked. Inside Wheat's Volkswagen. In the parking lot of the DeKalb Holiday Inn.

The parking lot wasn't lit, fortunately, but the few wedding guests wandering around the lot were, which was equally fortunate: the booze-happy couples, strolling arm-in-arm (for support as much as affection) did not even begin to notice the two naked people in the Volkswagen, which was slowly pulling around by the lobby entrance. I had Wheat do a U-turn so the car would be facing the exit when we got back. We (meaning Wheat and me: Selma and Shaker were safely across the street, in Sambo's, watching) were to run through the lobby and out across the Holiday Inn court and into the pool for a quick skinny dip, then cut directly across to the parking lot (which connected with the court) where the Volks would be waiting, engine running, our clothes on the seat. And we'd be gone. The essence of streaking is speed, and the getaway should of course be as fast or faster than the streak itself.

We climbed cautiously out of the Volks. Wheat's skin was pale in the moonlight, and if that sounds romantic to you, guess again. Wheat was skinny in a bony way and while he didn't exactly look under-nourished, he didn't look healthy either. He was also pretty much without body hair, and looked like a big overgrown baby, except for one thing.

We stood there by the Volks for a few hesitant seconds, in the darkness, the pavement cool against our feet. Wheat opened his mouth to say something, but I stopped him with, "Don't."

"Don't what, Kitch?"

"Don't say anything about your mom."

"I wasn't going to say anything about my mom, Kitch."

"No?"

"I was going to say something about my car."

"Yeah?"

"I was going to say I hoped nobody steals it while we're streaking. I mean, we're leaving the keys in it and the engine's running and all."

"We won't be in there that long. Don't worry about it."

"Okay, but I hope nobody steals it, because if they do, my mom'll kill me."

And we were off and running.

We burst through the lobby doors and immediately ran into a wall of people, which was not a good beginning. Streaking is supposed to be fast, as I think I mentioned before, and running into a wall of people, all of whom were wearing clothes which of course tended to make Wheat and me feel out of place, didn't improve our speed a whole lot.

As a matter of fact, Wheat fell down.

I lifted him up by the elbows and we pushed through the people and light flashed brightly in our eyes. We were in the midst of what was apparently some sort of wedding picture being taken, the family of the bride or groom I supposed. Anyway there was a whole bunch of them, lined up across the lobby, blocking the entrance. At least that's what they were doing until we entered the picture and plowed our way through.

Then we were weaving and shoving our way through a mob of formally dressed wedding guests, who'd been crowded around watching the picture taking, including the old people and the five-year-olds, too, and boy, were they a noisy lot: hoots of laughter and outbursts of indignation and everything in between filled the room in one combined, overwhelming blast of bad, boozy breath.

But we managed to keep moving, clearing the mob of people and cutting off to the left, down a short hall with coin machines on one side and rest rooms on the other. Wheat was out front, bony limbs and cold-air-reddened rear flailing in front of me. Wheat ran with all the precision and grace of the Scarecrow in *The Wizard of Oz*. I was the Cowardly Lion bringing up the literal rear, covering myself. (I guess I was the world's first and only shy streaker. Not that anybody seemed to notice.)

The cold air was a relief, after the boozy, stale air of the lobby. It splashed us and felt like diving into a swimming pool. Soon we were across the court (which was fairly empty of people, as hardly anybody was swimming on this unseasonably cold summer night) and then we were both jumping in the pool, and the sensation was somehow reminiscent of running outside into cold air.

If I hadn't had "somethin' to hide" before, as Shaker had put it, I certainly didn't have now. Between the chilly air and the chillier water I was shriveled up like Count Dracula the morning after. I climbed out of the pool, covered myself again, with one hand (which was no trick) and ran.

I was now in the lead.

I was running fast as humanly possible, but at the same time listening for the sound of something falling behind me, namely Wheat. As slippery wet as he was, and being awkward as a paraplegic penguin to begin with, Wheaty seemed doomed to hit the deck before reaching the Volks.

And then Wheat streaked by me, like a track star

getting his second wind, and with the gas torch lighting of the pool area reflecting on our bare backs, we were like a two-man nude Olympics, cutting a naked swath through the dark blue cloth of the night.

Up by Wheat's car some dark blue cloth was cutting its own swath.

Cops.

I didn't know where they'd come from, or how they could've gotten here so fast, nor did I feel now was the proper time to ask.

Wheat didn't see them.

He was running with his eyes closed.

"Wheat!" I yelled, as I turned and headed back toward the pool.

And then finally, Wheat opened his eyes and saw them.

Too late.

He said, "Oooooooooooh shhiiiiiiiiiiiiiiiiiit!" and ran over one of the cops, knocking the cop down, and both of them lay on the pavement, spreadeagled. And of course Wheat had somehow managed to land on his back, so he lay there with arms outstretched with his baby-skin turning baby-blue in the cold air.

I was still running, watching over my shoulder as Wheat did his naked pratfall, and when I looked where I was going I saw the pool dead ahead. I swerved and almost slipped on the wet paving around the pool's edge, but kept my footing somehow and headed for the juncture of two buildings, buildings that housed motel rooms, figuring there would be some sort of exit there. I scrambled through a door and found myself inside one of those buildings, with an endless hall of motel room doorways stretching out before me.

I paused, just a moment.

And kept running.

Now, it's very smug of you to sit there and say, "Wasn't it foolish of him to run through that building!" All I can say in my defense is, it seemed like the thing to do at the time, and when the endless hall came to an end, I took a right and bumped into something.

I pushed up from the floor and looked into a very pretty, young face. Blond hair, dark blue eyes. She was wearing a bikini the same color blue as her eyes. She had very nice eyes. She had very nice everything.

I covered myself.

"Oh," she smiled. She was younger than me, eighteen maybe. "You must be going swimming, too."

"Er," I said.

"What happened to your suit?"

"Uh," I said.

"You don't have any suit on." She just seemed puzzled about it, nothing more. I wondered when her fresh, innocent look would dissolve into a bloodcurdling scream.

"Hide me," I said.

"Pardon?"

"Police are chasing me. I'm a streaker."

"Oh! A streaker! Do people still do that?"

"Can I hide in your room?"

"I wouldn't mind it, but what would my mom say?"

"Are you sure you aren't Wheat in drag?"

"Huh?"

"Never mind," I said, and glanced at her barely covered breasts and thought, *No, that isn't Wheat*, and suddenly it was getting hard to cover myself.

So I said, "Goodbye," and started running again.

"Goodbye!" she said. "Hey! What's your name?"

"Fred!"

"Maybe we'll run into each other again sometime!"

"I hope so!" I said, smiling back at her, and kept running.

I didn't run into anyone else, and down one other hall I found an exit.

And a cop.

And then, pretty soon, I was riding in the back seat of a police car, sitting next to Wheaty. Both of us were still naked. Our clothes were stacked in the front seat, between the two cops. Neither of them was very old, the cops I mean. One was about thirty, the other in his mid-twenties. The guy in his mid-twenties turned around and grinned at us and said, "I got to hand it to you dudes. You got guts."

And the guy driving said, "Not brains . . . just guts." He was the cop Wheat had knocked over. He seemed a little gruff and slightly humiliated, where his younger partner seemed only to be mildly amused.

"Does he mean anything special by that, Wheat?" I whispered.

"What's going to happen to us," Wheat said. "What's going to happen to us."

"Wheat . . . is something going on I don't know about?" And all of a sudden Wheat's hands were moving. "You know what wedding that was? You know what wedding that was?"

"Wheat, please don't say everything twice."

"You know what wedding that was?"

That made three times, but forget it. "No," I said. "What wedding was that?"

"Nobody's. Nobody's. Just the police chief's daughter's, that's all."

"Oh," I said.

Suddenly I felt naked.

The cop behind the desk looked up at us, noted what we weren't wearing, then looked at the two cops who'd brought us in and raised an unimpressed eyebrow.

The cop Wheaty had knocked over (whose identifying name badge read BURDEN) said, "Streakers."

"No kidding," the desk man said. His face was as rumpled as the seat of a bus driver's pants.

Our clothes were under Burden's arm. He didn't seem to want to let go of them. He said, "Shouldn't we take a picture of these guys?"

The desk man shrugged. "I got the Playmate of the Month hangin' in my locker, Burden, but if you're into that, be my guest. To each his own."

Burden's face reddened and he said, "I'm going down and have a smoke, do what the hell you want with 'em," handed our clothes to the younger, friendly cop (whose name badge read FRIENDLY, coincidentally—I wouldn't lie to you) and stalked out.

The desk man said, "Touchy, ain't he?"

Friendly said, "He's just in a bad mood 'cause this big guy here knocked him down."

"You don't mean these girls resisted arrest, do you?"

"Not exactly. Anyway we're not gonna charge 'em with that."

"Pictures," the desk man said, shaking his head, returning to his paper work. "Give 'em their clothes and get 'em out of here."

"Hey, now, Sergeant, Burden may just be right about that. Taking pictures, I mean. The Chief's gonna want this handled right."

"Why," the desk man asked, looking up from his paper work with the strain on his patience obvious, "would the Chief give a damn about these two particular streakers?" He said the word "streakers" with the expression of a man holding up an especially smelly sock by two fingers.

And Friendly explained why the Chief would give a damn about these two particular streakers.

And the desk man got a Polaroid out of his desk and took our picture.

Then Friendly took us in the captain's office, which was empty (empty of the captain, that is: there was some furniture, of course, desk and chair, plaques on the wall) and gave us our clothes.

It felt good to be dressed again.

I said, "What's going to happen to us?"

"Tonight? Probably nothing. Not unless you don't have enough cash to post bond."

"I got my check book."

"That'll do."

"Then what?"

"Court tomorrow morning. A fine of some sort."

"What sort?"

"Maybe a hundred bucks."

"Each?"

"Each."

"What happens if we don't pay?"

"Don't as in won't, or don't as in can't?"

"There's a difference?"

"Listen, I'm no lawyer. You should talk to a lawyer."

Wheaty shouted suddenly. "Nobody gave me my rights!" He was waving his hands around. He looked like Hamilton Burger in the process of getting the legalistic crap kicked out of him by Perry Mason. "What about my rights," he was saying, "what about my rights."

But they didn't need to give us our rights for what they wanted to know. Out in the other room again, they asked for our name, address, date of birth, Social Security number, did we have $10 each to post the necessary percentage of bond?

I gave them a check for both of us, and wondered if I'd be going through all this again tomorrow, when the check bounced.

Wheat was over at the drinking fountain when Friendly came up to me and said, "Listen, do you know any lawyers?"

"Sure. We rent from a guy who's a lawyer. Real nice guy. What's all this talk about lawyers, anyway? What do we need a lawyer for, in a deal like this?"

"Because the Supreme Court ruled that a judge can't give a jail sentence to anybody not represented by counsel."

"Jail sentence?" This time I was the one waving his hands around. "Who said anything about a jail sentence?"

"The judge might," Friendly said. "It's not likely, unless he wants to be a real S.O.B. and really make an example of you."

"You mean we could actually go to jail?"

"Probably not..."

We went to jail. We did not pass go. We did not collect $200.

We owed $200. (The $100 fine each was the part of Friendly's prediction that *did* come true.)

The jail was a big double-story brick building built around the turn of the century. I had driven by that building dozens, perhaps hundreds of times since moving to Sycamore. Sycamore is only five miles or so from DeKalb, and is a quiet, little town, a restful retreat from DeKalb's busy university campus. Wheat and I sought Sycamore out after a bad first three years of college, divided between dorms and a frat house; actually it wasn't that the three years were bad, but that they were so good: so much fun, with both Wheat and me giving our all to playing cards and other social activities, and lip service to studies.

So we'd moved to more secluded digs at the beginning of the school year, in an attempt to keep our four years of college from stretching into five or even six. We had a nice basement apartment that we rented from a terrific couple named Nizer, whose door was always open to us. They were always willing to help out, and Mr. Nizer was more than willing to go to court with us. Unfortunately, Mr. Nizer, while a bona fide lawyer (of the corporate type), is not named Louis, which brings us back to the jail.

While I had driven by the jail countless times, I had never really looked at it before. It didn't look like a jail unless you looked at it close. It didn't look that much different from the nearby city hall, or an old school house, or any old double-story brick building.

But when you look close you can see bars on the windows. And when you see bars on the windows of a building, that's a real good sign the building's probably a jail.

Wheaty and I were going to jail.

But I'll tell you something funny: Wheaty did not get irrational, did not wave his hands or talk about what his mom might think if she knew he was going to be incarcerated for a month. No. Wheaty only starts waving his hands and talking about his mom and all when he gets flustered. There is no telling what will fluster Wheaty: it can be just about anything, anything that's at all confusing, or disorienting. But everything today was happening in a smooth, orderly fashion, go to court, be released into the custody of a correctional officer from the DeKalb County Jail (the jail located in Sycamore because Sycamore is the county seat) and go with the officer to the jail. So Wheaty was not flustered.

He was, in fact, fascinated by the whole experience.

And as we were walking up the sidewalk toward that ominously looming structure, Wheat said, cheerfully, "Gee, I never been to jail before, Kitch."

Like, "I never been to Boy Scout Camp before."

Then, once we got inside the front door, the place *really* got to looking like a jail. There was an electric lock door made completely out of tall, thick iron bars, and we were buzzed through and taken upstairs by the correctional officer and we were booked.

Yes, booked.

Isn't there a show on TV that always ends with some self-righteous cop glaring at the shifty-eyed crooks and saying, "Book 'em!" Dramatic phrase, right? Ever wonder what booking actually was? Maybe they take the crooks in back and beat 'em silly with a bound book of statutes; or put 'em on the lineup or other exciting things.

We got booked, and it was a bore.

Or anyway *I* thought it was a bore: Wheaty was enjoying himself. He especially liked getting fingerprinted and having his picture taken. That much *was* like TV: they really did put us against the wall and took front and profile shots while we held up something with our numbers on it.

Everything else was paperwork.

We filled out white cards with red lettering on them.

We filled out white cards with green lettering on them.

We filled out white cards with black lettering on them, too.

It was a lot like the information we'd had to give out at the police station, but a little more elaborate, and at the police station we'd only had to give it once, verbally, not write it down ourselves endlessly.

Somewhere along the line we were searched for dangerous weapons. Between us, the closest thing to a dangerous weapon was Wheat's Volkswagen key.

And then we were taken into a locker room and told to strip. "But isn't that why we're in here?" asked Wheat.

"Ummm," the correctional officer said.

All along we'd had the same correctional officer with us, a guy in his thirties with five o'clock shadow (and it was only mid-morning, remember) and eyes as blue as Paul Newman's (or Robert Redford's). He was very remote. Not nasty, just distant. Every now and then Wheaty would ask him a question and the correctional officer would say, "Ummm." No matter what the question. What time is it? Ummm. What year was this jail built? Ummm. How long you been at this job? Ummm.

Wheaty, naturally, did not notice that the correctional officer wasn't really answering. Wheat assumed he and the correctional officer were having a conversation.

And now Wheat looked at the correctional officer's uniform, which consisted of pale blue shirt with shiny badge, dark blue tie, dark blue trousers, no gun. And Wheat said, "Do we get uniforms?"

Remember we were standing there naked at the time.

"Ummm," the correctional officer said.

And kind of kicked at our clothes, which were neatly piled on the floor at our feet.

So we put our clothes back on.

I would have preferred having a uniform, frankly, and I know Wheat was very disappointed about not getting one. He said so. "What's the use of being in jail if you don't get a striped suit?" (He said this to me, later, having learned his lesson, finally, about talking with Ummm.)

Both of us were wearing nicer, less comfortable clothes than we normally chose to wear. We had dressed up for our court appearance, very clean-cut college boy short sleeve shirts and pressed slacks. We looked like a couple of models in a Sears catalog, not DeKalb County Jail's latest cons.

And then something remarkable happened.

Wheaty asked a question and the correctional officer actually answered. Made a sentence.

Wheaty asked, "What happens now?"

And the correctional officer said, "Now I lock you up."

"Ummm," I said.

Remember how I mentioned the jail, from the outside, looked like any big old brick building, an old school house maybe, the major difference being bars on the windows? The same was true of the inside. It was very similar to the junior high I went to in the seventh grade, same creaky floors, same grim pastel plaster walls. By grim pastel I mean all those nauseating institutional grays and greens society reserves for its criminals and school children. Of course the junior high I'd attended had been condemned and torn down six years ago, while DeKalb County was taking the more patient route and waiting for the jail to fall down under its own steam.

We were taken to a place called the Bull Pen, which in no way reminded me of my old junior high. This was the real thing: a large oblong room enclosed by heavy iron bars, bars stretching from floor to ceiling. Around the Bull Pen, which was about twenty feet wide and seventy feet long, was a catwalk, and around the catwalk were more iron bars, on three sides anyway: the back wall was just that, the back wall of the jail itself.

We were given individual cells within the Bull Pen. There were only six such cells, five of which were filled, now that we were there. The six cells were all in a row, and took up about a fourth of the Bull Pen. The rest was an open area (although there was a shower and a sink and all the necessary toilet facilities at one end) and in that open area were three large metal tables, which were sort of like picnic tables, although this wasn't my idea of a picnic.

But then it wasn't my idea of a jail, either. On the way over I had envisioned a drunk tank, the sort you see in the movies, a huge cage where scrufty, bearded derelicts lurk, looking for somebody clean to throw up on: a filthy pit with the toilet out in the open and with no seat on it, and no place to sleep but on the bug-infested floor. Instead, I found myself inside a dormitory of sorts, despite the iron bars and cement floor; a clean, orderly-looking place where two men sat at a picnic type table and played cards, while another sat nearby watching television (which was up high, beyond the bars, out in the catwalk area), all of them very ordinary looking guys, wearing street clothes. All in all, it was much better than I had expected, especially considering the rundown condition of the jail itself.

Still, it was nothing to write home about, and I was getting irritated at Wheat, who was walking around the Bull Pen with a grin on his face, looking the place over with the tickled expression of a new home buyer.

I went to my cell. It was, like all the other cells, pretty good size, and had a double bunk; had two people been required to make use of this cell, which was the intent of its design, it would have been cramped. For a single person, it was almost roomy.

Privacy was another nice feature. Blank metal walls were on three sides, the "front door" of the cell being bars and looking out on the area with the picnic tables.

So I had privacy when I wanted it, and company when I wanted it. Who could ask for anything more, other than to be able to walk out of there.

Wheat stuck his head in my cell, said, "Anybody home?"and came in and sat on the lower bunk. "This is really far out, isn't it?" He was glowing.

"Far out?" I said. "Far out? Look around you. See this light bulb in the wall here? Notice the wire mesh around it? That's so we don't take the bulb out and break it and use it to kill somebody. Do you notice anything funny about your shoes? That's right: they took our shoe laces away from us. Our belts, too. That's so we don't hang ourselves. Did you notice we're surrounded by not one, but two, count 'em folks, two rows of iron bars. Wheat. Haven't you noticed? We're in jail!"

"Well," Wheaty said, getting up off the bunk. "I don't see why you have to be in a bad mood about it."

I just looked at him.

He said, "I'm going out and meet the guys. Want to come?"

Meet the guys?

The guys?

You mean those four criminals out there?

"Okay," I said.

The guy watching television was named Peabody. He was a little pot-bellied man who wore wire-rimmed glasses and was around thirty-five years old. He wore a short-sleeve blue Banlon golfer's shirt and brown slacks. His hair was dark and receding. He looked more like an accountant than a criminal. We asked him what he did for a living. He told us he was an accountant. He told us we looked more like college students than criminals. We told him we only looked like criminals when we had our clothes off. He didn't seem to catch that. He was watching a soap opera he'd been following since he entered jail twenty-seven days before and told us, out of the corner of his mouth, that as soon as his stories were over (he followed various soap operas till four o'clock in the afternoon) he would get better acquainted with us. I could not imagine what he could be in for, unless he had embezzled or something else of a clerically criminal nature, but the county jail didn't seem a likely home for an embezzler.

"He's in for beating the crap out of his wife's boyfriend," Elam said.

Elam was one of the two guys playing cards. He was a friendly, self-confident guy with a wide, quick smile that seemed to me a bit sinister, at first anyway; later on, when I got used to him, it was just a smile. He was dark: dark complexion, dark hair, dark eyes, dark personality. He scared me a little, though he wasn't a big, thug sort of person. Not that he was short or skinny or anything, it's just with a guy like Wheaty around nobody else seems big, outside of maybe a palm tree. The scary thing about Elam were those eyes of his: they were kind of large, kind of pop-eyed looking, probably due to some sort of thyroid condition, though I never asked.

The other guy playing cards was named Hopp. That was his last name. I never did hear his first name, or Elam's either, for that matter. And as far as they were concerned, Wheaty was just Wheat, and I was Kitch.

And Hopp was Hopp. A heavy-set, sour-faced guy who never said much besides, "Deal the cards." He looked like Don Rickles, but even balder.

I had the idea Hopp could kill you with his bare hands if he wanted to, and had the idea too that Elam would stick a knife in a buddy's back for a dollar and a half.

"He also beat the crap out of his wife," Elam continued, still referring to the accountant named Peabody who, two tables away, was studying the television set with the concentration of an advanced yoga student.

"How long's he in for?" Wheat asked.

"He got sixty days. All he does is watch those soap operas, which are the story of his life, you know? Wives cheating on husbands and vice versa and people beating the crap out of each other over it."

"But he's such a little guy," I whispered. Peabody seemed wrapped up in his soap opera, yes, but I whispered just the same: I wasn't taking any chances getting a guy who beat the crap out of people mad at me.

"Yeah, well, his wife and her boyfriend were little, too. And he used a putter on 'em, sneaked up on 'em while they was together and tried to *putt* 'em to death. Ha!"

Hopp said, "Deal the cards."

They seemed to be playing a rummy game of some kind. I didn't recognize it, so it must've been a pretty obscure variant, I figured. There aren't many card games I'm not familiar with.

"Are his wife and her boyfriend okay?" I asked. Still whispering. "I'd think you could get hurt kind of bad by a guy hitting you with a putter."

"He'd of done a hell of a lot better with a two iron, I clue ya. Ha! Go fish, Hopp!"

"Go fish?" I said. "You guys are playing 'Go Fish'?"

"Yeah. We been playing worse than that. We played Crazy Eights yesterday, if you can believe it. We been playing everything two guys alone can play, and neither one of us likes this two-handed baloney, lemme tell ya. And the accountant over there won't play. He's got his 'stories' to watch. Ha! You boys play cards?"

"Uh," I said, smiling a little. "Do they, uh, let you gamble in here?"

Lunch was vegetable beef soup, barbeque pork sandwich and orange Jello with banana slices and marshmallows. And milk. "I love this place," Wheaty said. Slurping his soup. "This place is better than Howard Johnson's."

For once I agreed with Wheat. The soup was great, and the sandwich was no slouch, either. And while I'm not much on Jello salad, as Jello salads go, this one wasn't bad.

Elam, who was sitting next to Hopp across the table from us, said, "The sheriff's wife does the cooking. She's a real honey. Nice looking broad, too."

Hopp said, "You been in here too long."

Sometimes, when he wasn't playing cards, Hopp said things other than "Deal the cards," but it was always sort of startling when he did.

"What about dessert," Wheat said. "Do we get dessert?"

Elam nodded. He spoke as he chewed his Jello salad. His teeth and the Jello were just a shade different in color. "Wait till you taste the homemade doughnuts in the morning. Melt in the mouth. Best jail I was ever in."

"But isn't it kind of, uh, run down?" I asked. "I mean, are most jails in this bad a shape?"

"Hell, kid, you don't know when you got it good. Don't you know a jail with personality when you see it? This jail's been around. Half of Capone's boys spent their summer vacations in this joint."

Wheaty said, "You mean Chicago gangsters stayed here?"

I said, "In the DeKalb County Jail? How come?"

"Cook County Jail got so overcrowded, some of the neighboring counties had to take the overflow. My uncle was a bootlegger back then, told me all about it. Some of the people in charge here was on the take, so Capone's boys got the regular red carpet treatment. I understand they used to let 'em out to go get a beer, take in a movie, go out on a date. Ha!"

"Lace curtain jail," Hopp said.

"Huh?" Wheat said.

"Yeah, that's right." Elam said. "They called this place the lace curtain jail, 'cause the Prohibition crooks got treated like royalty. And you know something? We're treated that way ourselves. Good food, friendly guards, lots of privileges, and that Bull Pen with its big cells and TV and tables and decent toilet and shower, if that ain't home away from home I never saw it. Take it from me, I been in jails. This one's a honey."

"Even if it is falling down," I said, not fully convinced.

"*Because* it's falling down," Elam said. "The people running this jail, the sheriff for example, who has to live in here himself, feel so damn guilty about havin' to run a rattletrap old place like this, feel so damn sorry for us poor slobs stuck in here, why they bend over backwards makin' us feel comfy. Now you take a modern jail, all shiny and spit and polish, hell. The people running those places get to feeling like their tenants got it *too* good, got it *soft*, like a guy should feel lucky to be staying in such a nice looking new place with its chrome crappers and all. Ha! I tell ya something else, you get the worst damn chow in those places. Worse than army chow. You won't find food like this in a new jail."

We were eating downstairs, in a cell block similar to the Bull Pen but larger, with twenty cells (a row of ten on either side of the room) and bigger metal picnic tables than we had upstairs, two of them, where we'd been seated for the meal, the food already on the tables waiting for us when we got there. Three other prisoners joined the five of us from the Bull Pen for this and subsequent meals. A guard stood out in the catwalk and watched us eat.

Peabody, the accountant, was eating with a black guy at the other table. The black guy was small, skinny, boyish looking. He was probably about twenty. He was wearing a gray tee shirt and jeans. Peabody and the black guy were talking a mile a minute. It looked like they were planning a break or something.

Elam saw me watching them and said, "Hey. Don't stare at those guys."

"Huh? Oh. Sure. I didn't mean to, uh . . ."

"That little spade's a killer. He could have a temper. They got him in a separate cell. He's in for killing his wife's boyfriend."

"Oh," I said. Somewhat shaken. "I, uh, see why he and Peabody hit it off so good. They have something in common."

"Hope to shout they got something in common," Elam said. "They're both soap opera freaks. The spade's got a portable TV in his cell. That's what they're jabbering about, their soap operas."

Wheaty said, "My mom watches soap operas."

"Well," Elam said, "if she comes to see you visiting day, you'll have to introduce her to Peabody and the spade."

Wheaty was too busy eating his Jello to catch Elam's good-natured sarcasm. Wheat just said, "My mom's not going to come visit. I'm not telling her I'm in the clink."

"The clink," Hopp said.

Elam said, "I take it this is the first time either of you boys has been in the, ha!, clink. Do I guess right?"

We said yeah.

"So what are you in for? Now. You don't have to say if you'd rather not. First, lemme point out Hopp and me are generally bigger-time than county jail, know what I mean, but we lucked out, if you can call being stuck in the, ha!, clink, lucky. We got caught with some TVs in the back of a van. The van was ours, the TVs weren't. We got a year. We got another thirty-six days and then we'll be back to chasing a little bit more profitable rainbows than TV sets. I even got a particular little rainbow in mind."

Elam, like most thieves (he said), had a straight profession to fall back on, or use as a cover if need be, and his was short-order cook, though he had aspirations toward gourmet-style cooking. (Hopp's straight profession was piano-tuning, although on no occasion did he reveal any interest in or leaning toward anything at all musical; and all I could think of, when Hopp told us he was a piano-tuner, was that scene in *The Godfather* where a guy gets strangled with piano wire, which fit Hopp's image a lot closer than anything musical.)

"Why are you guys in the county jail?" Wheat asked, having finished his Jello and tuned into the conversation. "How come you guys didn't get sent up the river?"

"Up the river," Hopp said.

"Normally, yeah, I guess we'd been, ha!, sent up the river. But see, any sentence of a year or under is served in the county jail. Had we got a year and a day, it'd been prison."

I whispered, "Then why's that black guy here? Didn't he get more than a year for, uh, doing away with his wife's boyfriend?"

"Doing away with," Hopp said.

"The little spade didn't get nothin' yet. He's waiting to go to trial. You wait for trial in county jail. Prison's after that. So. What are you boys in for?"

I tried to think of a way to change the subject. I didn't know what a couple of tough guys like Elam and Hopp would think if they found out we were just college kids who'd been railroaded over a harmless prank. If they found out we were just punks, maybe they'd beat us up or rape us or something, and I would much rather just play cards with them.

But Wheat said, cheerfully, "We streaked the police chief's daughter's wedding reception."

And Elam laughed, a loud, uproarious laugh.

And Hopp smiled.

It was the first time I had ever seen Hopp smile, and it would prove to be a less than frequent event.

Elam said, "You guys are okay. That's about the

best damn reason I ever heard of for being in jail."

"Well," I admitted, "I guess it does beat beating up your wife and her boyfriend with a putter."

After lunch, metal tubs of hot water were brought in and set on the metal tables, and some towels too, and we washed and dried the dishes we'd just used. And I enjoyed doing it.

Because finally Wheaty had found something about jail he didn't like.

"I don't mind jail," Wheaty said, "but this washing dishes is punishment."

Wheat was beginning to get flustered. He was waving his hands around. Some soap suds flicked onto Hopp's shirt.

Hopp showed his teeth. And he wasn't smiling, either.

He spoke.

He said, "Settle down."

Wheat dropped his hands. They clunked on the bottom of the metal tub like stones. Soap suds flicked onto my shirt.

"Kid," Elam said, using a curled soapy finger to summon Wheat closer.

Wheat, mouth open, eyes white and round, leaned closer.

"Take it from me, kid: don't bitch."

"You mean you like washing dishes?" Wheat asked.

"Ha! I love it. You will too."

And we did, eventually.

What Wheat and I didn't know, having been in jail for only a few hours, was the boredom factor. You see, the bad thing about being incarcerated is not being stuck inside: most everybody spends the better part of the day inside one building or another, and if it's a factory or some other place where you work, you aren't really free to leave or go outside whenever you want, so it's not so different from jail or prison.

The bad thing about being incarcerated is boredom. Having nothing to do.

A typical day in jail consists of waking up in your cell about six, showering, going down to breakfast at seven, coming back and sitting in the Bull Pen, going down to lunch at twelve-thirty, coming back and sitting in the Bull Pen, going down to supper at five-thirty, coming back and sitting in the Bull Pen, shower again if so inclined, and going to sleep in your cell about eleven.

In the Bull Pen we could play cards or watch television. We could read, but no magazines or newspapers: we had to settle for the hardcover and paperback books available in the jail's library downstairs. We could have pencils and paper. There was a monopoly game. A radio. We could take naps. We could go to the toilet. And that's about it.

Maybe that doesn't sound so bad to you.

Maybe you're saying, "Well, it sure beats working." Try it.

You will find that any slight change from the norm,

any minute deviation from the Bull Pen's boredom, you will jump at. You will find yourself looking forward to doing your daily laundry. You will find yourself hoping the guards will say, "Today you guys can do some mopping downstairs." You will cling to the moments, after meals, when you are allowed to go down to the basement and use the candy machine and cigarette machine. You will smoke cigarettes, even if you never smoked before, even if cigarette smokes gags the hell out of you, as it does me. You will play ping pong for an hour after lunch, because a ping pong table has been provided for you and you damn well take advantage of it. You will wash your hands twenty-five times in one day. You will drink enough water to make a fish say, "Come on now." You will find yourself looking forward to the damnedest things, things that, in the normal world, you could never, ever imagine yourself looking forward to.

You will find yourself looking forward to doing dishes.

The next day, after lunch, a guard named Tobin, a sad-looking, middle-aged man who seemed as sorry to be here as we were, peeked through the Bull Pen bars and said, "Kitchen. Somebody to see you."

I looked up from my cards. We were playing pitch. Wheaty and I were partners. I had bid three and was having trouble making it. I immediately threw the cards in, went over to where the guard was looking in and said, "Fine."

And then it hit me.

Visitation was allowed twice a week. On Tuesdays and Saturdays. This was Tuesday.

Okay.

Visitation hours were one to three in the afternoon. It was now a little after two.

Okay.

Only immediate family are allowed to visit prisoners. Don't panic, I told myself. Maybe it's Mr. Nizer. Maybe they allow lawyers to visit, too.

I said, "Do they allow lawyers to visit?"

"Yeah," the guard said.

"Is it Mr. Nizer, my lawyer?"

"No," the guard said.

One down, three to go. Arlene?

"Who . . . who is it?"

Will the mystery guests please sign in:

"Your parents," the guard said.

I moaned.

"What d'you say?" the guard asked.

"I moaned," I said.

"You know where the windows are? I'll bring 'em over to the one on the right."

I knew where the windows were. Visitation windows. There were several of them, which opened up so you could talk to your loved ones without bars between you. Personally, I wouldn't have minded the bars.

Through the bars I watched my parents come into the catwalk.

"Awk," Wheaty said, from over at the metal table. "It's your folks!"

"Shush!" Peabody, the accountant, said. "Keep it down!" He was watching one of his soap operas.

Meanwhile, I was entering my own.

I looked out the window at my parents.

My father was wearing a black suit and a black tie. He looked like he was in mourning. My mother was wearing a summery, cheery bright-color dress. She did not look like she was in mourning: she *was* in mourning. She was crying, sniffling, dabbing at her eyes with a hanky.

I looked through the window and said, "Er, hi, Dad. Mom."

"Is that all you have to say?" he said.

My father is on the tall side, a lean-faced, kindly eyed man with dark brown widow's-peaked hair. He didn't look particularly kindly right now, however. I told you he's a minister, didn't I? Well, I was glad I wasn't on Death Row and this was the minister brought around to set me at peace with the world.

"Dad, I don't really know what to say."

"Why in God's name did you take your clothes off and run through the DeKalb Holiday Inn?"

"Dad, if I had it to do over again, I . . ."

My mother made a whimpering sound in her throat.

"You don't have it to do over again, Fred," he said, somberly. "It's done. Over and done. It's something you'll have to put behind you."

That seemed to me a bad choice of words, but I

didn't say so.

I said instead, "I'm glad you feel that way, Dad."

"Of course I feel that way. What other way could I feel? It's the Christian thing to do. I believe in forgiveness. I believe in learning from mistakes and going forward. All I want to know is one thing."

"Yes, Dad?"

"Why in God's name did you take your clothes off and run through the DeKalb Holiday Inn?"

"Dad."

"Yes?"

I have never been particularly close to my father. He's always been kind to me. He has never struck me. He has always been there with fatherly words of advice whenever fatherly words of advice seemed called for. But he's always been sort of remote, and his love has always been, well, Christian enough, but not particularly warm. My mother I have always been closer to. Related to better as a human being. Unfortunately, she is a crier. Did you see *Love Story*? Maybe you cried at the ending, I don't know; a lot of people did; I thought it was a crock, but a lot of people cried when they saw that ending. My mother was one of them. She cried for a week and a half.

She was crying now.

Right now when I needed her to referee between my father and me, she was busy crying and I had to deal with my good but distant father as best I could.

I asked, "How did you find out, Dad?"

"The Lord is everywhere. You can't hide from

Him, son."

"Dad . . . now don't take this wrong . . . but you aren't the Lord. You aren't everywhere. How did you find out?"

My mother reached in her purse. She was still crying, so I figured she was getting a fresh hanky. She wasn't. She was getting a newspaper.

She held it up.

It was the front page of the St. Louis paper the folks subscribed to.

Wheat and I were on it.

Remember that photographer at the wedding? Well, he sold his picture of Wheat and me crashing through the bride's family. He sold it to a wire service for a thousand dollars. You could see both of our faces very clearly. And most of the rest of us, too, though certain more delicate parts had had to be airbrushed out somewhat.

There was a very humorous caption beneath the picture, having to do with two zany college kids streaking the police chief's daughter's wedding reception. You'll excuse me if I don't reprint that caption here, as I'm afraid I find it less amusing than most people.

My mother tried to hand the paper to me, and I told her, "They won't allow us to have newspapers." She folded it back up, put it back in her purse, resumed crying.

"Don't ask me to explain," I said. "It was stupid, and I got caught, and that's all there is to it. I didn't know it was the police chief's daughter, I swear, Dad. It was all a terrible mistake."

"A terrible mistake," he said. "What about summer school?"

"They said we could have school books in here, so Wheat and I sent requests to the college asking if we could continue our courses by correspondence, but . . . but the profs turned us down."

"So you'll have to go back in the fall."

"I guess we will."

"And did you think of that when you took your clothes off and ran through the DeKalb Holiday Inn?"

"No, I didn't."

"What *were* you thinking of?"

"I was thinking I wished I still had my clothes on."

"Being flip doesn't answer my question."

"Well . . ."

"It had something to do with gambling, didn't it?"

Dad knew my hobby was playing cards, and disapproved. I played for such low stakes that he rarely got angry about it, but he disapproved.

"Yes," I said.

"Someone bet you you could do it," he said.

"Not exactly. That's pretty close, though."

"Have you learned anything from this?"

"I learned to keep my clothes on in public."

"Do you find this situation funny?"

"No. I don't like jail. Wheaty seems to like it, but I don't."

"Then I hope you've learned something. I hope

you've learned not to break the law. I hope you've learned not to gamble. If I could feel you had learned not to gamble, I would feel better about this."

"I'm through with gambling, Dad."

"Good, good. You'll be glad to know we paid your lawyer friend, Mr. Nizer, paid him back for covering your $100 fine."

"That's . . . that's very kind of you Dad. And Mom. Do you know if Wheaty's parents know about this?"

"They get the newspapers."

"Oh. Yeah."

"They sent money with us to pay his fine. You can tell him. They'll be here next Tuesday to visit him. You can tell him that too."

"I will."

"Your sister is fine."

My sister Angela is twenty-six and lives in Portland, Oregon, with her insurance salesman husband and their kid, and my parents see her once a year, if they're lucky. How they knew she was fine was beyond me, unless they had talked to her on the phone about my taking my clothes off and running through the DeKalb Holiday Inn. After all, they get the papers in Portland.

"Do you want us to visit you again?"

"It was great seeing you, Dad. And Mom. But it's a long drive for you. Why not just write. I'd love to get some letters."

Mom smiled through her tears and said, *"Ghh-ghallnfll."*

She meant she'd write.

"Good, Mom," I said.

Then my father asked me some questions about life in jail, and I answered them, and things loosened up a little. Mom finally stopped crying, partially, and asked a few questions herself. It wasn't so bad, then.

Finally my father said, "We'll be going now. Don't forget what you told me."

"Uh, oh, sure, Dad."

"About gambling."

"Right. I'm through with gambling."

We said our goodbyes, and they left, and I went back to my cards.

Hopp said, "Deal the cards."

I was telling Wheaty about how we were famous, how we had our picture in all the papers. And of course Wheat's response had been, "My mom'll kill me," and I told him he'd get the chance to find out next Tuesday when she came to visit him. He then got uncharacteristically silent and morose and sat shuffling the cards repeatedly, shuffled the spots off 'em.

Elam was vaguely amused by it all and made a gently sarcastic attempt to cheer Wheat up, saying, "Don't sweat it, kid. Ha! Maybe that skin book for the broads, what is it? *Playgirl?* Maybe they'll offer you a thousand bucks, to pose for 'em, now that you're a star, who knows?"

Wheat brightened, said, "You really think so?" and kept shuffling.

And Hopp said deal the cards.

Wheaty dealt the cards.

We were playing pitch. We had played it all day yesterday, and all morning today, and we were working on the afternoon.

Pitch is a good game for a foursome, even if you're not in jail. I find poker somewhat boring with less than six guys, and bridge is no good unless you're playing with really first-rate players. I've been Wheaty's bridge partner before, and the game requires a little more patience than Wheat's willing to bring to the table.

Wheaty isn't much of a poker player, either. He doesn't bluff well. His face could be called a lot of things, but a poker face it ain't.

However.

He happens to be a very fine pitch player. The game requires skill, intelligence and a sense of adventure. Wheat has all those things. There are occasions in pitch when a certain amount of bluffing goes on, where you pretend to be holding a card you aren't, or vice versa, and Wheat holds his own there, too. Having a partner gives him stability and coolness. Whereas in poker, for example, where he's on his own, he tends to panic. In pitch, he's a master.

Elam and Hopp were pretty good, too, but we won most of the time.

Hopp proved to be a poor team player, for one thing. His temper was bad, his judgment too (he wouldn't bid when he should, he would bid when he shouldn't, things like that) but he and Elam had been together a long time as, well, business partners of sorts, and Elam understood Hopp well enough to compensate for most of Hopp's weaknesses. Elam and Hopp made use of body language, which is a nice way to say they stopped just short of signals, and they talked across the table outrageously: "I don't know whether I should bid," Hopp might say, and Elam might casually reply, "It's only money."

Which was, by the way, another reason why pitch was a good game for us. In order to gamble, we had to be a little careful. Obviously, the guards knew the possibility at least existed that we were gambling for money, but seemed willing to look the other way as long as we weren't blatant about it. Pitch is scored on a sheet of paper, and I served as bookkeeper and kept track of who owed what. If we'd played poker, for instance, we'd have to use matchsticks as chips and all that, and it would have gotten complicated. This way, a simple tally sheet did it.

We had settled the stakes that first day, when a guard wasn't around. A guard strolled around the catwalk once every half hour and recorded what each of us was doing, on a sheet on a clipboard; but we didn't have constant supervision by television monitor as some jails do. Sometimes Elam got talking about what he and Hopp did for a living, which was a little scary; Wheat and I would exchange nervous glances, and then study our cards.

Anyway, the stakes.

Elam had suggested ten/twenty, and Wheat and I had readily agreed. We usually played a little bit higher stakes with our frat brothers and other college friends: ten cents a bump, twenty cents a game seemed pretty penny ante, even for penny ante players like Wheat and me; we'd have preferred a quarter a bump, fifty cents a game. But Elam and Hopp had been here before we were, so they had a right to make house rules. And besides, we'd be playing for a month, and a month was long enough to build up good losses or winnings, even at ten/twenty. (Though in pitch, if teams are evenly matched, things tend to even out, usually, over the long haul.)

In case you don't understand the card game pitch, I'll explain just a couple of things to make all this understandable to you. Pitch is a game where you bid, and if you don't make your bid, you go down: you bump. It varies game to game, but the way we played it, if you won you didn't have to pay for the times you bid and missed. There are variations of pitch, but we played the four point variety (high, low, jack and game) in which you can bid anywhere from one to four. If you have a great hand and feel sure you can make all four points, you "shoot the moon" and, if you make it, you automatically win.

"I think I'm going to shoot it," Wheat said.

Hopp looked up sourly. "Shoot it then."

"I don't know," Wheat said. "I don't know."

"You only live once," I said. (We did our share of talking across the table, too.)

Elam said, "Last time you guys shot the moon, you got your picture in the paper."

But Wheat hadn't heard any of this. He was studying his cards like an archeologist trying to figure out some brand of particularly baffling hieroglyphics.

Finally he said, "Okay. Okay. I'm gonna do it. I'm gonna do it. I'm going to shoot it. I'm going to shoot the moon! I'm shooting it, you guys!"

"Keep it down!" Peabody said. Twice already he'd asked the guard to turn up the television.

So Wheaty shot it in diamonds and we made it. Easily.

There was a whole lot of shooting the moon that afternoon. I shot it once and made it, Hopp shot it once and bumped, and Wheat shot it twice and made it both times. We were really getting the cards. All Hopp got was glum. Elam's attitude was what the hell.

By the end of that evening, Wheat and I were, by my tally, ahead $1.50 each.

After I showered, I stuck my head inside Wheat's cell and said, "Some cards we were getting."

"I shot it twice and made it," Wheaty said. "I shot it twice and made it."

"I wonder why Hopp takes it so hard? It's just nickel and dime stuff."

"Some people like to win. I know I do. I shot it twice and made it!"

I was grinning. I couldn't help it.

"You know something, Wheat? You been right all along. Jail isn't such a bad place after all."

So we played a lot of pitch. At one point Wheaty and I were ahead $10. Then for a long time we fluctuated between one dollar and five dollars. That's each, of course. Hopp continued to be in a bad mood, but he never got violent or anything. He just would say, "Deal the cards," and give off sour vibrations and that was that.

The Bull Pen population stayed the same: just the five of us: Elam, Hopp, Wheat and me. And Peabody, the accountant. We never did get to know Peabody very well.

Downstairs was different. The faces at meal time weren't always the same. The black kid's trial got under way, but he still ate his meals with us, and heard how his soap operas were doing from Peabody; I think it was a week exactly before we got out that he got his ten years in prison and left, and Peabody seemed very lonely at meals after that. Sometimes there would be just a few of us, just basically the Bull Pen regulars and a handful of others in the jail (there were also women prisoners in jail, but we never saw them). Other times it would be fairly crowded, if the drunk tank had filled up; we had crowds for the Saturday and Sunday meals, usually, as a lot of drunk-and-disorderlies got tossed in jail on the weekend. We didn't pay much attention to the shifting faces at mealtime. We were a clique, Elam, Hopp, Wheat and me. We played cards together, after all. We lived here.

One day in jail was pretty much the same as the

next. Only the first few days, and the last few, really stand out distinctly in my mind. Oh, yes, there was that Tuesday when Wheat's folks came around. That stands out in my mind, too, though nothing much happened, outside of some yelling from Wheat's mom, though it wasn't as bad as Wheat had imagined it would be. But then, nothing could be.

The day before we got out, Hopp shuffled the cards and said, "Let's up the stakes. Double 'em."

Wheat and I exchanged muted grins, said, "Sure," simultaneously. Elam and Hopp were into us for five bucks each and we didn't mind giving them a chance to make their money back.

Elam said, "Hold it, Hopp. I can't see doubling the stakes. We're into these guys enough as it is."

Elam was kidding, of course, and Wheaty and I laughed, which made Hopp kind of mad.

"Okay, punks!" Hopp said. It was like somebody opened the door on a blast furnace. "Self-confident little smart-ass punks. You got the guts to play for a little more, or not?"

The laughter caught in our throats. We'd been around Elam and Hopp so long we'd begun to forget (or maybe accept) what they were, which was crooks. My first impression of Hopp, remember, was that he looked like a killer. I'd gotten used to him, considered him kind of a grouchy comedy relief, a Wheaty in reverse: short and fat and unhappy and harmless. But I all of a sudden realized that one element of that equation was off-kilter: that Hopp was Wheat in reverse, all right but Wheat was the one who was harmless and Hopp, well . . .

Hopp slapped the metal table with his hand and it was like he'd hit it with a trowel. The sound was a kind of pinging echo bouncing off all the bars around us.

"Well?" he demanded.

Elam said, "Hopp. Cool off, man. We're all friends here. Ha! What the hell? Why not sweeten the game up a little bit? It's only money. You guys willin'? Okay. Twenty/forty she is."

That was in the morning. We won till eleven o'clock. By lunch we had hit the even up point. After lunch we kept on losing. It was all downhill. We never rallied. They weren't cheating us or anything: the odds were just catching up with us. We'd had nearly thirty days of predominantly good cards. It was time for a losing streak.

We kept playing trying to climb out of it, ending up throwing good money after bad. We played most of the evening. We lost $15 each.

Neither of us felt too terribly bad about it. After all, we were getting out of jail tomorrow.

Hopp's reaction, however, was rather intense. For Hopp, that is.

He went around smiling, which was unsettling.

I hadn't seen the sun for thirty days. It was good seeing it again. It hurts to look at the sun, you know, but I did anyway, and loved it. Looking at the sun is just one of the many trivial things that seem important after you've spent time in jail. The sky is very blue in the summer, in the Midwest, and the clouds are very white. I studied them. Wheat was doing the same.

Walking outside in fresh air—not the stale, supposedly air-conditioned stuff we had breathed inside—was pleasurable beyond words. It took us half an hour to walk the couple blocks back to the apartment at the Nizer house. We would just stand on a street corner, breathing, feeling the hot sun on our skin, looking at cars drive by with pretty girls in them. Not all the cars had pretty girls in them, of course, but a lot of them did, and a lot of girls seemed pretty to me today that maybe wouldn't have before I went to jail for thirty days.

Next door to the Nizer house is a carry-out food place, a minor league chain restaurant that combines elements of several of the major leaguers, selling fried chicken, hamburgers, ice cream, you name a kind of junk food and this place sold it. The place was a huge plastic-looking red barn with a four-foot statue of a chicken on top.

Between us we had a few dollars left from what we had taken with us to jail (Mr. Nizer had loaned us twenty bucks each to spend on cigarettes and candy and what-not, while we were inside) and we proceeded to order and eat five cheeseburgers and two double malts and a pound of French fries between us. Wheaty ate one more cheeseburger than I did, but I ate more French fries than he did.

The food at the jail had been good, but we had developed an insane craving for some nice, greasy junk food. And the nice, greasy junk food at this particular carry-out joint was served by some very young, very pretty girls in short white dresses like nurses wear in cheap sexy movies.

Maybe you've guessed by now that pretty girls are another of the not-so-trivial things you miss spending time in jail.

As we sat and ate our cheeseburgers and malts and fries, Wheat said, "We're gray."

"Huh?"

"Our skin is gray."

"No it isn't. What do you mean, our skin is gray?"

"See for yourself." He held out a hand as evidence. It was not gray. It was largely yellow and red, being smeared generously with mustard and ketchup.

"What are you talking about, Wheat?"

"You skin's just as gray as mine is. Everybody's skin's gray after they get out of prison."

"We weren't in prison, Wheat. We were in jail. And we weren't in jail long enough for our skin to turn gray."

"What would you call it, then? The color our skin is."

"Pale. Regular pale skin color. Eat your cheeseburger."

"Here it is summer. The middle of summer, Kitch! We ought to have real nice tans by now."

"It's hard getting a real nice tan in the Bull Pen."

"I know. Your skin turns gray in there."

"You're incredible. You loved jail, while you were in there! Couldn't get enough of the place! Now that you're out, you're complaining. You're something else."

"I guess you're right. I guess I am going to miss the old Bull Pen at that."

"Wheat. Forget what I said. Go ahead and complain."

I was in no mood to wax nostalgic about that hole. I was in a mood to revel in sun, cheeseburgers and pretty girls.

"Come on, Kitch. Admit it. You enjoyed yourself. All those cards. Even if we did end up losing."

"Aw, I was getting tired of playing cards. Give me the salt."

"Here. The hell you were tired! You never get tired of cards. You'd play cards tonight, Kitch, if ya got the chance."

"You're wrong there . . . no more cards this summer. Sun and fun, that's where it's at."

"Now you're talkin'!"

"Only . . ."

"Only what, Kitch?"

"Only I suppose we really ought to get out and find ourselves some jobs. We're going to have to raise the cash for school this fall. And it won't be easy finding a summer job at this late date."

"We could go back and work at my dad's store, back home." Wheaty's dad is manager of a furniture

store, which is where we had worked for a year between high school and college.

"Think he could use us?"

"He always runs a big sale in August, Kitch, you
know that. He'll be able to use some extra help."

"And till August rolls around, sun and fun?"

"Sun and fun."

We toasted malt cups.

"We'll call Dad tonight," Wheat said. "Collect. You
know something, Kitch? I'm gonna kind of miss our
ol' pals Elam and Hopp. What a couple zany guys."

"Zany? Zany? Those guys are crooks, Wheat!
Didn't you hear what they were saying? That they
knocked over this place and that? Those guys are
robbers."

"Well, for robbers they're a couple zany guys.
They weren't such bad company."

"I for one am glad I'm not going to be seeing either
one of them again."

"But we are gonna see them again, Kitch."

"What d'you mean?"

"They'll have to come around in a week, when
they get out, to collect the money we owe 'em. We'll
see 'em then."

"Yeah. I suppose you're right at that. They'll come
for their fifteen bucks a piece we owe 'em is right.
What the hell. Maybe they'll stay for some cards."

There was a police car waiting for us. Pulled in behind
Wheaty's dust gathered Volks in the Nizer driveway.

It was a very familiar-looking police car. So were the two cops sitting inside, motor running, windows rolled up, enjoying the air-conditioning. Friendly was driving this time, and Burden, who had spotted us walking up, rolled his window down and leaned his head out and said, "Get in."

For a moment I thought Wheat was going to make a break for it.

He had this panic-stricken look in his eyes and I caught his elbow and whispered take it easy.

I said to the cops, "What do you guys want?"

"Just get in," Burden repeated.

"This is Sycamore," I said. "Do you have jurisdiction here?"

Wheaty said, "We want to see our lawyer, you guys."

"Just get the hell in the car!" Burden said. "It's hot out, and the longer I got to talk to you smart asses with the window down, the hotter it gets!"

We got in.

"We haven't done anything," Wheat said. "We just got out of jail."

"Don't get so excited," Friendly said. "Keep your shirt on."

"We'll keep our shirts on," I said. "We shower with our shirts on these days. We're reformed. So why don't you just tell us what this is all about?"

Burden turned and looked at us—at me, in particular, wilting my burst of tough guy courage—and put a disgusted sneer on his face and said, "Shut your smart-ass traps. The Chief wants to see you."

"The Chief?" I said.

"The Chief?" Wheaty said.

"The Chief," Burden said.

"The Chief," Friendly said.

The DeKalb Chief of Police whose, daughter's wedding reception we had nakedly disrupted wanted to see us?

Burden said, "You don't have any objections, do you? To seeing the Chief?"

"I want to see my lawyer," Wheat said. "I want to see my mom."

I said, "We don't have to go with you. We haven't done anything. We're getting out of this car, right now."

Burden flicked something on the dash that locked our back doors, and then proceeded to back out of the alley and drive toward DeKalb.

We didn't go to the police station. We went to a residential area, a nice, quiet, upper middle-class neighborhood, with a lot of shade trees lining the streets and big houses with big lawns. Not mansions, but not exactly prefabs. We pulled up in front of one of them, a white one with black trim. A heavy-set guy in a yellow sportshirt and tan shorts was watering the grass in the front.

At Friendly and Burden's bidding, we got out of the car and walked across the big green yard.

The Chief was not a good-looking man. His head looked small for his body; his facial features looked big for his head. Receding gray-black hair, bushy eye-brows over rather bulging gray eyes, fat round nose and a wide mouth, the sort that smiles all the time but never really does, really.

"So," he said.

His voice was low. Rumbling bass.

"So," I said.

Wheat said nothing.

"So you're the boys who took their clothes off at my daughter's wedding reception."

"I guess so," I said.

Wheat said nothing.

"Got some publicity out of it, didn't you?"

"We didn't do it for publicity, sir," I said.

Wheat said nothing.

"What did you do it for?"

"What did we do it for?"

"What did you do it for?"

So I told him briefly, of our gambling debt to Shaker and how we'd paid it off, and that thirty days in jail, the hundred dollar fine and losing out on summer school had been punishment in spades for what seemed to us a relatively harmless prank.

"I agree with you," the Chief said.

"What?" I said.

Wheat said nothing.

"That's why I asked you boys here today."

I didn't point out that we hadn't been asked: that we'd been brought.

"Come on inside and sit on the porch with me and

have some ice tea."

It took a few moments for the invitation to sink in.

That low, rumbling voice of his sounded sinister even when he was being friendly. Finally, we followed him to his porch, took tall glasses of lemoned, faintly sugared iced tea and sipped tentatively, half expecting the drinks to be spiked with something lethal.

"You pulled a bad judge, boys," the Chief was saying, sipping his own iced tea. "A real hardnose and I want you to know the harshness of that sentence wasn't any of my doing."

"That's . . . that's nice to hear, sir," I said.

Wheat said nothing.

"As a matter of fact," the Chief said, "I really brought you here to tell you thanks."

"Th . . . thanks?"

"Yes. What I'm going to say now is strictly confidential, you understand . . . but actually I'm grateful to you boys for streaking through that reception. It made my little girl's wedding a wedding to be remembered. She thought it was wonderful!"

"Wonderful?"

"Great sense of humor, that little gal. And how many girls have their wedding reception written up in papers all over the country? The President's daughter, but who else? So, we're delighted, my little girl, her mama and me. Of course, officially, I have to be outraged. I hope you can understand that. For example, because the wedding photographer sold that picture of you to that wire service, I threatened to sue him . .

. since that picture legally belongs to me, having paid him to take pictures, after all . . . and he settled out of court. Gave me back all the money we'd paid him to take pictures, and that thousand bucks he made, too. He still came out good, from the publicity. Anyway, I wanted to thank you. I can only say I'm sorry that you boys couldn't have fared as well as we did in this affair. At least you can have the peace of mind to know that as long as you're in this area, you don't have to worry about the police chief bearing a grudge for what you did. I feel bad about the thirty days. It's a crying shame. More tea?"

"Uh, no thanks," I said.

Wheat said nothing.

"If you boys ever need anything, he said, "just holler. And thanks again. You can find your way out, can't you?"

We found our way out.

The cops took us back to Sycamore.

Friendly and I chatted about the weather, politics, baseball. Burden grunted an opinion now and then. Wheat said nothing.

Finally, after we were back to the Nizer place and the cops had gone, Wheat turned to me and said, *"Thanks?"*

So everything seemed to be falling into place for Wheaty and me, for a change. First, there was the DeKalb Police Chief not being mad at us, which had initially stunned us, then relieved us, and finally amused us. Second, Wheat's father had come through with the furniture store job, meaning we'd make enough money during the month of August to come back to the University and finish up those few courses in the fall. And third, the Nizers, who were going on vacation to Colorado, gave us the key to their lake home in Wisconsin, in return for doing some minor, menial repairs and painting and such around the place, after which we'd have plenty of time to pursue our visions of sun and fun.

Other, less-earthshaking blessings were heaped upon us by a temporarily merciful providence. For one thing, Wheat's Volks didn't overheat on the drive to Paradise Lake, where the Nizer lake place was, despite a day so hot we almost longed for the air-conditioned jail. Almost. And for another thing, we were able to *find* Paradise Lake, which is one of the least developed and most hard to get to of the many lakes in that area, though I think it's unfair of Wheat to call it "Paradise Swamp," and I'm sure he was just kidding when he pointed over to the wet, weedy vacant lot next to the Nizer cottage and said he saw an alligator crawl out of there.

The cottage itself, though, was pretty nice, by Wheaty's standards or anybody else's. It was an A-frame with two bedrooms, one up and one down, and lots of burnished wood paneling, with early American furniture and a somewhat incongruously modern kitchenette, with a microwave oven we cooked TV dinners in. We did all the repairs and painting the first day. We spent Thursday and Friday chasing girls at the beaches at nearby Twin Lakes and Lake Geneva.

Late Friday afternoon, Wheaty and I were sitting in the high-ceilinged living room of the Nizer cottage, drinking Olympia beer (which is Clint Eastwood's favorite brand, by the way, all us two-fisted types drink Oly, you know), discussing where we would go that evening in pursuit of pretty girls, when somebody knocked at the side sliding glass doors.

"Wonder if that's the girls from last night?" Wheat mused aloud.

"Maybe," I said, and went to answer it.

I drew back the drape that covered the glass door and it was Elam and Hopp standing out there on the sun-dappled porch.

"Hey!" I said smiling, genuinely glad to see them. I was glad to see them because jail was already fuzzing up in my mind, an experience viewed through the soft-focus camera of memory, turning those thirty days into an interesting, youthful experience that would make for some funny anecdotes in the years to come. Also, I was glad because I was on my third Oly.

I slid the door open and they came in.

Wheat jumped out of his soft chair. "Elam! Hopp!" It sounded like he was speaking a foreign language. "Come on in, you guys! It's good to see ya!"

Hopp said, "Where's our money?"

I said, "Uuuuh?"

Wheat said, "Whaaa?"

Elam said, "Hopp! Ease off, man." He turned to

us, and smiled. And for the first time since that day I met him in the jail, his smile seemed sinister to me, again. "Listen, boys," he said. "You got to excuse Hopp here. We got a little hot driving up in this heat. Those lousy back roads! Ha! Bitch to find this place."

They did look hot. Hopp was wearing faded blue working pants and a gray muscle-man shirt that had sweat circles under the arms the size of pie pans. Elam was wearing a yellow sports jacket, a dark blue silk shirt, white pants and a bulge under the left arm.

Hopp held up a fist that looked like he was holding up a rock.

He said, "Where's our money?"

I said, "Whaaa?"

Wheat said, "Uuuuh?"

Elam said, "Hopp's just hot, don't mind him. But he's right. We did come after our money. And it does look like you're kinda hidin' out from us. Not that we think you kids would even think of runnin' out on your old pals. Ha! Who'd think that?"

"Why would we want to run out on you?" I asked. I didn't know whether to be scared or confused. I settled on both.

Wheat said, "You guys came all the way up here to collect a crummy fifteen bucks?"

"Fifteen bucks?" Hopp snarled. "Fifteen bucks my butt! Who you trying to kid?"

"Awright, awright," Wheat said, staying remarkably cool.

"Fifteen a piece, I mean. Thirty crummy bucks, I

mean. So what's the big hairy deal?"

"The big hairy deal," Elam said, "is the fifteen hundred bucks each you owe us, pals. The three thousand bucks you owe us."

Wheaty dropped his can of beer.

So did I.

Where was Clint Eastwood when we needed him?

Wheaty laughed. Or maybe he whimpered. "You guys," he said. "Cut it out, you guys. You got some crazy sense of humor, you guys. Stop kidding around."

Elam said, "Maybe you haven't noticed, but Hopp, he don't kid around a whole bunch."

"Why, uh, why don't we all sit down," I said, motioning to the two semi-circular couches that faced each other in the middle of the room. "I'll, uh, get us some beers." I picked up the cans Wheat and I had dropped and headed for the kitchenette area.

Wheat followed me. He said, "What is going on? What's going on?"

I was opening the refrigerator. "Are they sitting?"

"What?"

"Glance back there. Are they sitting?"

"Yeah. Yeah, they're sitting. What is this all about, Kitch? Three thousand bucks, Kitch. What kind of joke is that?"

Wheat's hands weren't moving around yet, but panic was clearly setting in.

I handed him two Olys and said, "Don't get upset."

"Who is upset? I don't see anybody upset. Do you

see anybody upset? I wish my mom was here."

"Wheat. Cool. Stay cool."

"You're shaking, Kitch. You're telling me stay cool, and you're shaking. How can I have confidence in somebody who's telling me stay cool and is shaking?"

"Will you just settle down? And when we go back in there, don't say anything. I'll do all the talking."

"You'll do all the talking. Just tell me one thing, Kitch . . . do you know what's comin' off here or not?"

"I think I do."

"Really? No kidding, really? What?"

"I think we do owe them three thousand dollars."

Wheat dropped the beer cans I'd handed him. These two were still unopened, fortunately, so it didn't make a mess. He sat down at the kitchen table. His mouth was open. His eyes were as glazed as the stale doughnut over on the counter where he was staring.

Well, that was better than waving his hands around a hundred miles an hour. I guess.

"Hey!" Elam's voice boomed, from out in the living room area.

Wheat jumped a little.

Me too.

Elam continued: "What the hell's taking so long? Get your butts in here!"

I led Wheat by the elbow, and juggled four beers and managed to get Wheat sat on the couch, across from Elam and Hopp, and got the beers distributed all around. Elam and Hopp popped the tops on the beer cans and Wheat and I jumped a little, again. I opened the top on my own can and handled it better. Wheat left his can unopened. He was just sitting and staring, like out in the kitchen. Elam's sinister smile had faded, replaced by a frown that made me nostalgic for the smile. Hopp's eyes were narrowed in his face, like a couple bad cuts that hadn't healed.

I sat next to Wheat.

"There's been a misunderstanding," I said, with a smile even I did not believe.

I paused for Elam to say, "How's that?" But he didn't.

I pressed on. "It's uh, really quite amusing when you think about it." I laughed a little.

Hopp said, "Get on with it," after which his lips pressed back flat together, making his mouth look like a gash in his face, going well with the festering sores that were his eyes.

Lord, was I scared.

But I had a speech to make, and I made it.

"When we set the stakes for our pitch game, at the jail," I said, "we just said 'ten/twenty,' and everybody said fine, remember? But Wheat and I are penny ante players, and we assumed you meant ten cents a bump and twenty cents a game. We didn't stop to think that you guys are higher-stakes players than we are, that you play in games where the table is literally littered with ten- and twenty-dollar bills. We didn't stop to think that maybe you meant ten dollars a bump and twenty *dollars* a game."

Wheat said, "Awk."

I said, "Easy, Wheat. Easy. Anyway, that's what happened. . . . Wheat and I thought we were playing penny ante. You guys thought the stakes were, uh, a little higher. But . . . excuse me . . . but you guys are at fault, too, I mean, you should've known just looking at us that Wheat and me aren't exactly high rollers. So, uh, everybody's, you know, at least partially at fault? So, uh, can't we just call it an honest mistake on all our parts, and uh, shake hands friends and . . . forget about it?"

Silence.

A year passed. Or maybe it was a minute. Anyway, I was a year older.

Finally Hopp said, "You're going to pay."

Which was an ambiguous thing to say. I mean, he could have meant that a couple of ways.

But I didn't bother asking him to clarify.

Elam said, "That's a real interesting story . . . but I just bet if you boys had come out the winners in that game, you'd be wanting to be paid off in dollars, not pennies."

Hopp nodded. "They planned this all along."

Elam said, "The pitiful part is, I thought you were a couple of nice kids. I liked you. Ha! I guess you got to be careful about making friends in jail."

"Please," I said. "Be reasonable. Look at it from our point of view. We're not con artists. We're just a couple of college kids who landed in jail because of a prank."

"Ha! I thought you were in jail 'cause you took off your clothes and ran through a motel lobby."

"Yes!" I said, seeing a straw and grasping at it. "And do you know why we took off our clothes and ran through that motel lobby?"

" 'Cause you're a couple of anti-Establishment hippies or somethin', how the hell should we know?"

"Elam. Hopp. We owed this guy seventy-eight dollars from a card game, and couldn't afford to pay him off, and he said if we streaked through the Holiday Inn lobby, he'd forgive the debt. I mean can't you see that two guys who can't afford to pay off a seventy-eight dollar debt, who'll do something crazy and ridiculous and illegal and even land in jail because they can't afford to pay off a seventy-eight dollar debt, aren't too likely to have three thousand dollars lyin' around to pay off another debt, which they got gambling in jail, where they landed after doing something crazy and ridiculous and illegal because they couldn't afford to pay off a seventy-eight dollar debt? Hah?"

Hopp spoke to Elam but looked at us. He said, "Give me your gun. I'm gonna kill 'em."

Wheat fell off the couch.

Just because Wheat and I were making fools of ourselves, dropping our beers on the floor, falling off the couch, don't get the idea we were fooling around. It may read like slapstick comedy, but it lived like something else. Maybe you think the expression "scared silly" is just an expression. It isn't. Wheat and I were fools out of fear.

While I was helping Wheat off the floor and back onto the couch, Elam was telling Hopp to take it easy.

"You take it easy," Hopp said. "I say they got to pay." This time it didn't sound quite so ambiguous.

And then Elam said something very corny. He said, "Dead they aren't any good to us."

It was a corny line from a corny movie, and in a corny movie you would never take it seriously.

I took it seriously.

Wheat had that glazed look on his face again, was just sitting there like a big hunk of wood, and I for one was glad. I had enough to contend with just trying to deal with Elam and Hopp, let alone having to manage Wheat's behavior.

Elam said, "Let me explain something to you boys. Let me explain something about gambling debts. Hopp and me are from Chicago. Grew up in the same neighborhood, and drifted into . . . business, together. We got lives of our own, of course, Hopp's got a wife and five kids to support, and I got a lady friend who's more expensive to take care of than that. It's expensive period, livin' in Chicago. Cost of living is somethin' you wouldn't be-*lieve*. But we get by, Hopp and me. Got to work our butts off to do it, though. We're on the road a lot. Mainly what we do is knock over a bank here and there."

My heart was a triphammer. I hadn't been this worked up since I streaked through the DeKalb Holiday Inn. Elam was confirming suspicions I'd gathered spending time with Hopp and him in jail, but hearing him come right out and say, "We knock over a bank here and there," was very disturbing. And put teeth in Hopp's threat to kill us. Furthermore, my bladder was killing me.

"When Hopp and me get ourselves in a card game," Elam was saying, "we take it serious. We play a lot of cards in Chicago, and we mess around with other kinds of gambling, too, only we aren't just messing around. I like the horses, but Hopp, he leans toward dice. He's a more physical type than me, I guess. Maybe you noticed. Anyway, when you gamble in Chicago, at least in the circles Hopp and me move in, you get in big trouble if you don't pay up. In fact, you don't even think of not paying up. Ha! Not for long, anyway. What you do, if you owe some guy some money, is you borrow some money from some other guy. You don't go to a bank, 'cause bankers get upset when you ask for a loan to pay off a bookie. Besides, I try and make it a rule never to go inside a bank without a gun in my hand."

"Why . . . why are you telling us this?" I asked, not wanting to hear any of it at all.

"Don't interrupt. Anyway, where was I, oh yeah... that money you borrow when you can't pay off a gambling debt, that's called juice money. You know what that is, don't you? You know what a shylock, a loanshark is, don't you? Weekly interest going on forever, till you can pay off the principal? Good. Anyway, Hopp and me both owe this guy some money. We were out on the road, trying to pull off a couple deals that would give us some coin to pay off this guy, when we got tossed in the can. While we was in, our bill with this guy is goin' wild as a pervert in a nudist camp. How could we make payments while we was in jail? So we owe this guy a lot of money. We can't go home again."

All of a sudden he was quoting Thomas Wolfe. "What do you mean?" I asked.

"We can't go back to Chicago and Hopp to his wife and five kids and me to my lady friend till we can pay off this damn shylock."

"What's that got to do with Wheat and me?"

"You owe us three thousand. That would've been enough to get this guy off our backs a while and let us go home. We been in jail a year, boys. We want to go home."

"Well, gee," I said, suddenly feeling guilty, "I'm awful sorry. I mean, we really weren't trying to put anything over on you . . . I can understand how disappointed you must feel."

Hopp started to lurch toward me but Elam threw an arm over Hopp's chest and held him back.

Elam said, "I believe you, boys. I believe you when you say you misunderstood what the stakes were in our game. But that don't change anything for Hopp and me."

Hopp had settled down a little, after making his lunge and being halted by Elam. He said, "Whose Volkswagen is that outside?"

"My mom's." Wheat's voice was very tiny, incongruously so coming out of his big hulking frame.

"Your mom's?" Hopp said. "What's she doing here?"

"Is she here?" Wheat said, round-eyed. "Where? Where?"

I said, "It's Wheaty's car. It's in his mom's name, that's all."

Hopp said, "I don't give a damn whose car it is, we'll take it back and sell it."

Elam said, "Ha! That thing isn't worth five hundred."

"It is so!" Wheat said, and I shushed him.

"Maybe," Hopp said, and began what was the closest thing to a speech I ever heard come from those thin, menacing lips, "we could go rent a U-haul truck and back it up to this place and haul everything away. There's no neighbor on either side. It'll be dark soon. Some of this stuff looks like antiques to me. And the kitchen appliances and all would help. What do you think?"

What I thought was that the Nizers would feel we had somewhat taken advantage of their hospitality, if we aided Elam and Hopp in looting their lake home, but I had the good sense not to say anything.

Wheat didn't.

He said, "That'd be stealing!"

Everybody looked at him. Hopp especially.

He said, "But if you guys think it would be best, well . . ."

Elam said, "No. This antique stuff is a pain in the butt getting fenced. For all the work it'd take emptying this place, we'd come up with peanuts. And some of these lake areas are patrolled pretty regular, 'cause there's a lot of vandalism and burglaries in any area where you got homes that aren't in use all the time, cottages like this one, that only get used on good weather weekends. No. Bad idea."

"You got a better one?" Hopp said.

"Better isn't the word." Elam said, and his sinister smile returned. "Winning," he said, as if it were a magic word.

"Winning?" Hopp said. "That'd take three men, at least!"

Elam nodded toward us.

Hopp got this skeptical look on his face.

Elam said, pleasantly, "How would you boys like to work out what you owe us?"

Wheat and I exchanged a worried look. We had thought, from the way the conversation had drifted, that Elam and Hopp (or anyway, Elam) had accepted the concept of our not owing them anything except $15 each.

I said, "I won't be involved in anything illegal."

"Me either," Wheat said. "Streaking's where I draw the line."

Elam blew air out of his cheeks, thoughtfully. "Okay," he said. "I got to talk to Hopp alone for a minute. We're gonna go over there a minute and then we'll be right back. Okay?"

We nodded.

Then they were over whispering in the kitchenette, and Wheat said, "I got to go to the bathroom."

"Join the club."

"What do you think they're talking about?"

"I don't know. Whatever it is, I don't like it."

"Maybe you didn't realize it, Kitch, but I was scared crapless through all of that."

"Really? You sure covered it well, Wheat."

"Maybe, but all I know is one thing."

"What's that?"

"I'm not ever gonna get involved with those guys in anything again, without first knowing the stakes."

Which is one of the smartest things I ever heard Wheat say.

I only wish one of us had been listening.

Elam and Hopp returned from the kitchenette and took their places on their semi-circle couch and faced us. Hopp tried to smile. He didn't show any teeth. I never saw any of Hopp's teeth in my life. But he did try to smile, I'll give him that much. It came off as a fold in the fabric of his face, which was better than a gash, I guess. Elam's smile was sinisterly unsinister, if you can follow that. Or maybe I was just getting paranoid.

Judge for yourself.

Elam said, "Let me tell you about a little town a few hundred miles from here. In this little town is a little bank. The bank is really just a sort of store-front operation, small, single room. A branch office of a bank from another, little bit larger town nearby. You'd think in such a small town, with less than a thousand people, the bank wouldn't keep much cash in its vault. You'd be wrong. Because this little town has nearly a dozen businesses. Of course the business district, if you can call it that, isn't much . . . one city block, on one side of the street . . . a little grocery store, an appliance store, a tavern . . . and you know it's a little town if there's only one tavern! The other side of the street is taken up by a filling station that's next to, or I guess is part of, a repair shop that does more farm machinery repair than auto, and sells farm machinery too. On the north edge of town there's another filling station, with a cafe. Between the filling station and where that little business district I told you about starts is a grain elevator, a lumber yard and two feed stores. On the other side of the little business district is a Shell oil storage depot, with all kinds of trucks that make all kinds of deliveries in the area. And what that all adds up to is that for a little branch office bank in a little bump-in-the-road town, that bank has some *pre*-tty heavyweight depositers. Maybe ten, fifteen thousand in that vault, on a weekend. Watched over by a staff numbering two. A manager, and a teller. Ten, maybe fifteen thousand dollars, and two employees lookin' after it. I tell ya, it's a crime."

That was what I was afraid it was.

And I said, "I know what you're leading up to, and I won't be part of it. I am not . . . *we* are not . . . no matter how you threaten us . . . going to take part in robbing a bank."

"Robbing a bank!" Wheat said. "What bank? Is that what he's talking about? Robbing a bank? My mom'd die."

"You might keep her company," Hopp said, forgetting about trying to smile.

"Hey, now, everybody hold on a second," Elam said. "I'm not asking you boys to help Hopp and me rob that bank. Not exactly."

"Not exactly?" I asked.

"What, do you think I'm crazy? Do you think I'd take a couple of college kid amateurs on a heist? You boys don't exactly impress me as a pair that holds up well under pressure. I like the people I work a job with to be a little less high strung than you two."

"Then why," I asked, "are you telling us about this bank that's begging to be robbed?"

"Robbing that bank'll take four men. It could be done with three, but four's better. Two guys who've worked with Hopp and me before are gonna be getting out of the Ft. Madison, Iowa, state pen in two weeks. We're gonna do the job with them. But first I got some preliminary work to do. I only got a, you know, fleeting glimpse of this little town, when Hopp and me passed through there one time after knocking off another bank in that same area. I kicked myself in the butt when I saw that little branch bank and all those damn businesses, hell. We'd just got something like six thousand from a bank three times as big, in a town big enough to have cops, and here maybe fifteen thousand was sitting, unguarded."

Wheat said, "You mean some towns are so small they don't even have a cop?"

"Some towns are so small," Elam said, "they don't even have a whore. So, anyway, I got preliminary work to do. Got to go in that town, in that bank, look things over."

"Case the joint, huh?" Wheat said.

"Case the joint," Hopp muttered.

"Yeah, right, kid," Elam said. "Except even more than that. See, I like having a trial run of a job before I actually pull it. It's a rule of mine. And that's where you come in, boys."

"No," I said, "it's where I go out. Wheat, too."

"Now listen to me," Elam coaxed. "Just hear me out. All I want you boys to do is fill in for those two friends of ours, who are in the pen and aren't handy for the run-through."

"Yeah, Kitch," Wheat said. "It's just a sort of dress rehearsal."

"Dress rehearsal," Hopp muttered.

"That's right, kid," Elam said, "you got the right idea. You just stick to the script I give you, and, well, pretend it's an actual robbery. Otherwise I won't be able to get a good idea of how the real robbery'll go."

"I won't be part of it," I said. "Of a robbery or a trial run or anything."

Elam unbuttoned his jacket.

"I don't care," I said. "Threaten all you want. I don't even think you have a gun under your arm, how do you like that? You just got out of jail. How could you have a gun? I'm too good a poker player to be bluffed, pal. So just run along. Just forget about it and go. Wheat and me will have no part of your bank robbery or anything else."

Elam opened his jacket a little, as if he was warm and wanted to cool off. The metal of the gun butt caught some of the light of the dying sun from the window behind me and reflected.

I reflected, too. And after reflecting I said, "It's not like you were asking us to be part of, uh, actually robbing the bank, I mean, it's just a run-through, after all. . . ."

I wouldn't have got in that car if I'd known it was stolen.

But I thought it was just a car. Just a car Elam and Hopp had arrived in at the lake cottage yesterday. Had I been thinking, and not just operating on automatic pilot, it would have occurred to me that Elam and Hopp had just got out of jail, and this car—a brand-new yellow Mustang—was a model that had not been on sale when Elam and Hopp went into jail a year ago, that had come on the market while they were inside, and since they were broke they couldn't have bought it yesterday, so of *course* it was stolen, what *else* could it be but stolen?

Only none of that occurred to me till I sat in the stolen car in Wynning, Iowa, in front of the Wynning branch office of the nearby Lone Tree bank, at nine o'clock in the morning, waiting for Elam and Hopp to come out.

We had come down from Wisconsin in a two-car caravan, Wheat and me in the copper-color Volks, following Elam and Hopp in the yellow Mustang. I could have made a break for it, I suppose. I probably should have. I think the reason I didn't was Hopp was turned around in the rider's seat of the Mustang up ahead of us, staring at us the whole time with a look so full of meanness Peter Lorre could have learned something from it.

Wheat was in a talkative mood, but I wasn't listening. He was alternating between excitement about our forthcoming adventure, and panic about said adventure's illegality; but he never got to the hand-waving and my-mom'll-kill-me stage, so I didn't try to calm him down or even bother entering into conversation with him. I just drove. I had that crystal-clear, wide-awake feeling you can only have when you haven't had any sleep for twenty-four hours; you are past being tired, and feel you are alert. You feel you are alert the way a drunk feels he's witty.

It had been dark when we started out. I'd watched the dawn as we drove through Wisconsin on into Illinois, and the morning was turning out sunny and blue-skied by the time we hit Iowa. Elam kept the Mustang at a steady fifty-five, taking no chances. That was fine with me: I was in no hurry, though at the same time wished to hell it was over. Finally, we crossed a bridge over the Cedar River and Elam took a side road turn-off, which was as expected, since his plan called for a side route into Wynning, rather than taking the regular turn-off a few miles hence.

Soon we were pulling in behind the yellow Mustang down a gravel drive that led to an abandoned farmhouse, a two-story clapboard gutted by fire and beyond restoration. A barn stood nearby, a paint-peeling, gray building that had been untouched by the fire but was badly sagging and apparently not being used or if so just for storage or something. I parked the Volks on the far side of the barn, so that the car could not be seen from the blacktop road that passed by the farmhouse.

We gathered together, beside the Volks, and Elam told us one more time what it was we were each to do. We were dressed casually, Wheaty and I in cut-off jeans and tank-top tee-shirts, Elam and Hopp wearing unusually bright Hawaiian print sport-shirts and light summer slacks. It seemed odd to me that Elam and Hopp would dress so loudly, and I pointed that out, but Elam explained that the attention of the bank employees would be drawn to the shirts, not the faces of the men wearing the shirts. There was, evidently, a lot of psychology in bank robbing. There was also a lot of attention to detail in Elam's run-through: Hopp was even going to carry the laundry bag into the bank, rolled up under his arm, the laundry bag that would be used to dump the money in on the real robbery.

Then I got in the Mustang, behind the wheel, while Elam got in on the rider's side and Hopp climbed in in back. We left Wheat behind with his Volks. All of this was according to plan.

A little more than a mile later we were in Wynning. The side route into town brought us through a middle class residential neighborhood of older homes, ranging from modest one-story clapboards (usually white, with a screened-in porch) to nearly elaborate two-story gothic types, and most of those were white clapboard too, but not always: a red brick house broke the monotony now and again, and some of the less conservative residents had dared to paint their homes a color other than white . . . you know, something really daring, like a washed-out pastel yellow. Glancing down side streets I saw that the town seemed to be nothing *but* middle class: the lowliest residence around was an occasional trailer, and those sat in large, well-tended yards.

I also saw a church, or maybe I should call it a chapel; it was Methodist, and I thought of my father, and squirmed.

And then the residential area seemed to end before it began, and we were sitting at a stop sign looking out onto the smallest, least active Main Street imaginable.

Down to the right I could see the lumber yard and feed stores Elam had mentioned, with the grain elevator looming behind them; to the left I could see the towers of the oil company's storage silos. In between was the world's smallest business district. On the side of the street closest to us was the filling station and garage, where farm machinery was repaired and sold, all of that taking up a small city block. Next to that, across a narrow street, was a city park, which was for the most part a green open area, with a few trees around the edges; there was a small band shell and benches in front of it. The park took up somewhat more space than the nearby filling station and garage, having some room to stretch out, as there was no street cutting between it and its sprawling next-door neighbor, the oil company storage dump. By normal standards, the park was small, but by the standards of this tiny town, it was huge, and I found it somehow refreshing that Wynning, seemingly a very business and industry-oriented little community, had set such a relatively large section of itself aside for a park.

Directly across from the park, but staggered somewhat so that it was also across from the filling station and garage, was the long single block that made up the bulk of Wynning's business district. On the corner straight across from us, as we sat at the stop sign, was the town's only bar. Next to the bar was a Clover Farm grocery store.

Next to that was a general store of sorts, apparently a hardware store as much as anything. Then came a large appliance store, and finally, on the other corner, the branch office of the Lone Tree bank.

All of these stores were old; none of them had had their faces lifted. The buildings were brick and the store-fronts were wood and glass. Old, but scrupulously well-maintained. Wynning had looked the same way in 1925.

And clean. The whole damn town was frightening-ly clean: you couldn't find a candy wrapper or crushed cigarette package to save your life.

We could see some cars parked down the street, at the cafe, but the curb in front of the bank and other store-front businesses was empty of cars. It was not what you'd call a hustling, bustling Saturday morning in Wynning.

I pulled up in front of the bank, not directly in front as Elam didn't want the two bank employees to be able to look out their big glass window and get a good look at the car, but back just a ways. The sidewalk was raised several feet, meaning there was a sort of wall as you got out on the rider's side, so I left some room, didn't pull in close.

That was when Elam told me the car was stolen, and to watch myself accordingly, and he and Hopp got out and went into the bank.

An Iowa Highway Patrol car drew up alongside of me and slowly slid into the space at the curb in front of the stolen Mustang. I shut my eyes. I opened my eyes. The Highway Patrol car was still there.

I hadn't even gotten over the car being stolen yet, and here was the Highway Patrol already! Terrific.

The patrolman who'd been driving climbed out. He was wearing a faultlessly pressed green-brown uniform, with a badge that the sun glinted off, a tall guy who was trim-looking, in a big-framed, supple, athletic way. He didn't look much older than me, which should've been a comforting thought, I suppose, but it wasn't: he looked very much like the sort of college jock who got a kick out of doing bodily harm to non-jock sorts like me. He looked very much like Shaker Saltz, as a matter of fact, who, in case you've forgotten, is the college jock S.O.B. who got me into all this.

And he was walking back to me. Kind of stretching, rolling his neck around, limbering up like a wrestler getting ready for a match. He was wearing sunglasses, the wrap-around goggle type, and the sun glinted off them, same as his badge. His teeth were shiny white and the sun glinted off them, too.

Only he wasn't smiling. He just had his lips pulled back across his teeth, getting ready to speak. To me. He pushed his Highway Patrol hat back on his head and let me look at the fringe of military trim blond hair on his tanned, shiny forehead. He leaned forward and said, "I notice you have an out of state license."

"YES!" I shouted. And realizing I'd shouted, grinned feebly, tried to disguise how hard I was breathing, said a prayer for my bladder, and repeated, with superficial calm, "Yes."

"What's wrong with you?" he asked, in a flat tone of a voice.

"Wrong? Wrong?"

"You nervous about something?"

"No, no, no, no, no, nervous about something? No."

He sighed. "Well you'll have to move your car."

"Move my car?"

"I would if I were you. Unless you're here for the day."

What was that supposed to mean?

"I'm waiting for a couple friends," I said. "They'll just be a couple minutes. I can move it then, if that's all right."

"Suit yourself," the patrolman shrugged, and walked back to his car and joined his partner.

I had no idea what was going on.

I was still upset about Elam's last-second revelation that I was sitting in a stolen car, and now, less than a minute later, here was a Highway Patrolman telling me to move that car, but was he *really*? I couldn't tell if he was *telling* me to move it, or *suggesting*. And why would a Highway Patrolman want me to move a car parked on the Main Street of Wynning, Iowa, on a Saturday morning, at nine o'clock?

I glanced around, looking for a clue. The street was still deserted. Had the street been cleared for some reason? I had just assumed—we all had just assumed—the street was simply quiet. Wynning was not exactly your teeming Metropolis, after all. The only signs of activity were some teenage kids over on the far side of the park, pitching a big tent, a tent big enough to hold a meeting in.

Was that somehow significant?

I stepped out of the car and took a look at the bank. Because of the raised-up sidewalk I couldn't see the bank from the car, hadn't really got any sort of look at it yet at all.

I saw that the venetian blinds on the store-front window of the branch office bank were drawn. I hadn't noticed whether they'd been drawn when we drove up or not. Maybe Elam and Hopp had drawn them; maybe that was part of their side of the run-through. They hadn't told Wheat and me any of the stuff that would happen inside the bank; we just assumed they'd go in there, get change for a twenty or cash a check or something, and, you know, just get a general look around at the lay-out of the place and all.

And then I noticed the "Closed" sign hanging in the window of the door. And the shade was pulled on that window, too.

What?

I knew that according to Elam's instructions I was to sit in the car with the motor running. I knew that Elam had insisted I stay put, and under no circumstances was I to enter or even approach the bank. But something was drastically wrong here.

I leaned back in the car, switched off the motor, and hopped up on the sidewalk.

They'd been inside four minutes.

I looked in the big store-front window, to the side of the venetian blinds, where there was just a crack you could see through to the inside of the bank.

I saw Elam standing in front of the teller counter with a gun in his hand. I saw Hopp behind the counter, standing in the doorway of the open vault, stuffing packets of money into the laundry bag. I saw the tops of the heads of two people, one man, one woman, both of whom were sitting on the floor behind the counter. They were apparently tied up and, I supposed, gagged.

I took two or three dazed steps back away from the window and turned around, head spinning, and said, "That's a trial run?"

The Highway Patrol officer on the rider's side looked up at me from his car and said, "Did you want something?"

"NO!" I shouted. And grinned feebly, and repeated, "No."

By now you must be wondering why these two Highway Patrolmen didn't find my behavior suspicious. I was wondering that myself. Evidently they thought I was just another nut who got nervous around police types, and let it go at that. Evidently they had other things on their minds.

Meanwhile, I stood there on the sidewalk teetering between the Wynning branch office of the Lone Tree bank and those two unpleasant vehicles, the Highway Patrol car and the stolen Mustang, wondering what to do. Oh, I had options, sure, but when your options revolve around a bank in the process of being robbed, a Highway Patrol car and a stolen Mustang, you find yourself unable to do much of anything, except maybe stand there on the sidewalk, teetering.

I considered just walking away. Hoofing it on out to that burned-out farmhouse where Wheat waited, Wheat and his Volks, Wheat and his beautiful, *not* stolen Volkswagen. It wouldn't be like I'd driven off and left Elam and Hopp behind. If I left the key in the Mustang's ignition, it wouldn't be like I'd left Elam and Hopp in the lurch.

Would it?

But suppose I did walk away. Elam and Hopp would come out of the bank with a bag of money in one hand and a gun in the other, and there could maybe be shooting, and did I want to be responsible for that? That would be like seeing an accident coming and not yelling "Look out!"

Furthermore, Elam and Hopp, teed off at me for deserting them, would probably immediately tell the patrolmen where to find Wheat and me.

I considered going over and telling the patrolmen what was happening inside that bank, but how could I? I was in this up to here. I was an accessory to a bank robbery, and still would be, even if I helped stop it mid-stream.

And suppose I did tell the patrolmen: there was liable to be shooting that way, too.

See what I mean about the options at hand? Did you ever see such a bunch of lousy damn options in your life?

Then it occurred to me that if I was not going to leave, if I was not going to turn my back on the bank and walk away, I at least had to warn Elam and Hopp. I had to tell them not to come out of there with that bag of money slung casually over their shoulders.

So, with what I hoped was a nonchalant air, I walked back over and tried the door to the bank.

Locked.

Well. That was no surprise.

I knocked. Softly. Not wanting to unduly disturb the patrolmen sitting drowsily in their vehicle nearby.

No answer.

That was no surprise, either.

I kept at it. I knocked a bit louder. Just a bit.

And finally Elam's voice, in a friendly tone, said, "I'm sorry, we're closed this morning."

"It's me," I said.

Elam cracked the door open.

"Take a look out front," I whispered.

Elam looked. There was an almost imperceptible tightening around his eyes, but that was all. He did not blow. He was too professional for that, I guess.

"All right, kid. Turn around and face the street. Fine. Now lean against the building there. Good. I'm going to leave this door cracked open just a shade so I can keep talking to you. I'm gonna have to keep it low, kid, can ya hear me okay?"

"Yes."

"Cover your mouth with your hand when you talk. Like you was yawning or coughing or something."

I nodded.

There was a pause, and he said, "I guess you know what we're doing in here."

"Yes."

"Thanks for sticking around."

"Go to hell."

"I know how you must feel, kid. When you get a

chance, think of it from our point of view and maybe you'll understand. For right now just hang loose a second and leave me think about this. Well. We obviously can't come sashshaying out of here with a bag of money over our arm, can we? So okay. We wait it out a while. We wait and see if the Highway Patrol is staying around for something, or just making a short stop to kill some time. If things stay the same for longer than fifteen minutes, knock on the door again, and I'll tell ya where we go from there. Got that, kid?"

"Listen, I'm leaving. The key'll be in the ignition. I'm going to walk out and join Wheat at that farm and get out of here. You can't say I ran out on you, 'cause I came up and warned you."

"Kid. Stick around."

I heard the door close.

And then the concession wagon rolled in. I was still standing on the sidewalk, just getting ready to get back in the Mustang and "stick around," like Elam suggested, when this dinosaur of a camper came rumbling down the street. The camper was white, but it was garishly painted with red, yellow and blue lettering that said, "El Tacomobile."

"Gooooooood Eats, Hombres."

"Burritos, Enchiladas and Tacos" and "Gringo Food, Too!" There were also bad paintings of little plump Mexicans wearing extravagant sombreros, sleeping under palm trees.

The Tacomobile pulled in two inches from the back

bumper of the Mustang.

My mouth dropped open, and not from craving a taco. I walked unsteadily around the Mustang (there was a space of half a foot between it and the Highway Patrol car, so I could just squeeze through) and took a look at the front of the concession wagon, or rather the side of it, the part facing the street. There was more garish Tacomobile lettering on the bottom half, and more plump Mexicans taking siestas under palm trees; but the upper half was unpainted, as if they hadn't gotten around to that yet, but then a panel dropped to reveal screened windows behind which food was cooked and served up and sold. The woman inside was a tiny middle-aged Chinese lady. Why was a Chinese lady running a Tacomobile, you ask? How should *I* know? I was busy wondering what a Tacomobile was doing pulled in behind the stolen Mustang, on an otherwise deserted street in Wynning, Iowa.

I was still wondering when the second concession wagon rolled in. It was much the same as the Tacomobile, only it was painted up differently. This one said "Cotton Candy,"

"Sno Cones," and "Lemonade," with poorly painted depictions of each. I mean, you had to sort of study it a while before deciding which picture went with which caption. I think the same artist did them as the Mexicans.

Along about then a band started to play.

From off in the distance. But not terribly far away, like from maybe two blocks. The song the band was playing was "Going Out of My Head," performed in the style of John Phillip Sousa.

A marching band.

But what were they doing?

They were marching. And playing. They marched and played their way from the cafe two blocks down and ended up right there, in their stiff blue uniforms, all twenty-some of them, high school kids and a skinny young director with a sissy mustache, standing in front of the Wynning bank, the Highway Patrol car, the stolen Mustang, the Tacomobile and the cotton candy wagon. And me.

When they stopped playing, I asked the Chinese lady in the Tacomobile what was happening here.

She answered me in Chinese.

Then the director dismissed the band from what apparently had been a rehearsal, and they loosened their hot little collars and scattered around the street, chattering, shouting, mostly swarming around the two concession wagons. I backed away in horror. Some of these creatures were girls, but in those sexless uniforms it was hard to tell if anybody was human or not. A good-looking majorette with blond hair and a skimpy sparkly uniform was over talking to the director, but otherwise I felt engulfed by faceless, sexless blue uniforms.

"I told you to move your car," somebody said, "and you wouldn't listen."

It was the Highway Patrolman with the dazzling badge, teeth and forehead.

"Well if you weren't here for the day before," he said, smiling that ugly smile you only find in people with no sense of humor, "you are now."

And he walked away.

Across the street things were starting to happen.

I noticed the tent I'd seen those teenage boys starting to pitch was pitched. Some people were in the park. Not many, maybe half a dozen, men and women both, wearing clothes too formal and hot for the day, walking around in circles and looking official, carrying clipboards, wearing square plastic name badges.

I heard a scraping noise. Like an eight hundred pound man scraping a hundred pounds of fingernails across a four hundred pound blackboard. But it was only the two Highway Patrolmen, lugging this thing out into the street, hauling this huge saw-horse thing, the type you use to seal a street off with.

They were using it to seal off the street.

"Oh brother," I said.

I glanced down in the other direction, to see if the street was sealed off that way, too.

It wasn't. It wasn't sealed off with a saw-horse thing. There was a bus, however, two blocks down, by the cafe, parked sideways in the street. The school bus the band came in, of course.

And over between the garage and the park, cars were parked in the street. Not along the street. *In* it. Cars belonging, apparently, to those official looking people wandering around the park with clipboards and plastic badges.

Right now one of those official-looking people, a male, was supervising while two of the teenage boys hung a banner over the entrance of the big tent.

The banner said:

WYNNING FOUNDER'S DAY — CENTENNI-AL CELEBRATION

There was only one thing I could think of to do. I bought some cotton candy.

When I was sure the two Highway Patrolmen weren't looking, I knocked on the door to the bank, then leaned against the building, eating my cotton candy.

I heard Elam's voice say, "Things are gettin' worse ain't they, kid?"

"Well better isn't the word."

The cotton candy made an excellent cover for my talking to Elam. And it tasted pretty good, too. Trouble was I was wolfing it down. I was nervous.

Elam was saying, "What is this, some kind of celebration?"

"Founder's Day. Centennial."

"Yeah, yeah, I can just make out the banner over on that damn tent. Ain't this a problem, though."

"Elam."

"Yeah, kid?"

"I'm leaving."

"Not just yet, kid."

"What's stopping me?"

"Just a second. I'll call Hopp over and let you ask him that."

"Never mind. You make your point. What do you have in mind?"

"We're comin' out. Like I said before, we can't exactly come outa here with a bag of money over our shoulder. Not at a time like this. So I figure we'll leave the money inside for now."

"Inside?"

"Right here in the bank. Can you think of a safer place? I'll get the key to the front door from the manager, and we'll just keep the bank locked up, for now."

And before I could question the logic of that move, the door had eased shut again and I was alone with my cotton candy . . . and the high school band, concession stands, Highway Patrol. . . .

A minute or so later Elam and Hopp strolled casually out of the bank, shutting the door (with its closed sign hanging in the window) behind them. Elam looked very cool. Hopp was a little wild-eyed, but probably not enough so to alert any innocent bystanders to anything unusual in his character. I had finished my cotton candy and didn't know what to do with the paper cone the stuff had come wrapped around. I certainly didn't want to throw it on the sidewalk, not with the cleanliness fetish *this* town had: getting busted for littering right now would've been less than ideal.

Elam gestured over toward the park, at the benches in front of the small bandshell. The only people in the park were the official types, their teenage helpers, and marching band members still taking five. Elam said, "Let's go over there and sit down a minute and relax."

That was a good idea. Relaxing was a terrific idea. I figured in a year maybe I would be able to relax again, but why not start trying now?

We picked our way through the marching band members who were standing and chatting and eating tacos and things in the street and sat on the bench in the first row in front of the bandshell, which was close enough to the edge of the street for the trees that surrounded the park to provide shade. So it was relatively cool there, in the shade, on those benches. Comfortable. Birdies were singing. Pretty shafts of sunlight came peeking through the shimmering green leaves of the trees. I thought I was going to barf.

And it wasn't the cotton candy, either.

It was Elam and Hopp and this snowball that had caught me up on its way down the mountainside in the process of becoming an avalanche.

"Ya look kinda pasty, kid," Elam said.

"Must be the cotton candy," I said.

Elam was on my right. Hopp on my left. They began talking through me.

Hopp said, "So what's the deal?"

Elam said, "We got to leave the money behind. For now."

"For now?" Hopp asked.

"Right. We can't stay around here much longer. This damn celebration, Flounder's Day or whatever, is gonna bring some people into this town, and unless we want to spend all day mingling with the crowd, we better get outa here."

"What about the money?" Hopp said.

"We'll come back for it. After dark. After this Centennial thing shoots its wad and the sidewalks of this Podunk get rolled up proper. We just pull up to the bank, use our key to get back in, grab the money and run."

"Can I say something?" I said.

Elam nodded. "But make it fast, kid."

"Somebody's going to miss those two bank employees. They're *bound* to be missed. If you come back here later, there'll be cops all over. Or a trap of some kind. That only makes sense. I think we should all get out and get away from here, while we can."

"No," Elam said. "That angle's took care of. Before we left, we had both of them bank employees call and say they wouldn't be home till late tonight. The girl was from Iowa City, single, twenty-four, lives with another girl who's gonna be gone the rest of the weekend, anyway. The man is from here, but he called his daughter and told her he was called out of town on business for the rest of the day."

"Oh," I said.

"What now?" Hopp asked.

"We walk out to that farmhouse where Kitch's goofy pal's got that car waiting," Elam said. "The important thing now is we do it before this celebration thing gets going full steam."

All during this conversation I had been playing with the sticky paper cone from the cotton candy, twisting it around my fingers like a dunce cap that was too small for me. Now, as Elam was talking, telling Hopp we had to get out of here, I spotted a trash receptacle by a tree nearby, and got up to get rid of the paper cone. I tossed it in the can and, as I turned to rejoin Elam and Hopp, I saw something.

I saw that the park had filled up with people.

Behind where we'd been sitting, the benches were full. People were sitting quietly. Quiet as church.

I sat back down between Elam and Hopp, and said, "Uh, don't look now, boys, but . . ."

Hopp said, "We gotta get outa here."

Elam said, whispering, "Cool it. Leave me think a second."

Up on the bandshell one of the official types, a man, was fiddling with a centerstage microphone. He was tapping it, blowing into it, even talking into it, anything to try and see if it was on or not, while another official type, a woman, stood out front to see if anything was coming out of the speakers. Finally, in the middle of a sentence, the official type on the stage discovered the mike was now on. His embarrassment (the part of his sentence that came out over the mike was ". . . wrong with this silly thing?") drew some titters from the crowd. Then the official type who'd been standing out front, the woman, hollered at one of the teenage helpers to adjust the amplifier, which apparently was off in the bushes somewhere. There followed some feedback and squeals and such until the microphone was adjusted properly.

What this meant, obviously, was that something official . . . a ceremony or presentation of some kind . . . was about to take place.

Elam, being no dummy, sensed this and said so.

Hopp said, "Let's just get up and leave before whatever this is gets started."

I said, "Good idea."

Elam's whisper turned harsh. "We're in the front row, you dummies . . .we got to be careful. We got to wait for just the right moment."

Hopp said, "The right moment is now."

I said, "I agree."

I figured the longer we waited, the more chance there was the show would get on the road before we could.

But Elam had his reasons for staying put. He jerked his thumb over toward the place where the park and the street met: the two Highway Patrolmen were standing there, with arms crossed. There was nothing in their faces to suggest they suspected us, or anybody, of anything. They looked bored, actually. Still, I could understand Elam's hesitation for calling attention to ourselves by getting up and leaving from these front row seats, with the entire town of Wynning sitting and standing behind us.

Up on the stage, five men sat in five chairs. The microphone was in front of them. They were dressed in suits and looked official, but in a different way than the clipboard, plastic-badge hurry-scurry bunch who'd been ordering teenagers around all morning.

These men had the look of say, a mayor and city council members. (Which is what they turned out to be.)

And then the sound of sirens shattered the peace and quiet of the park, like crazy people let loose, screaming.

They were police type sirens, and Hopp hopped to his feet the moment he heard them.

So did just about everybody else.

The five people on the stage jumped out of their five chairs. The townspeople sitting on the benches behind us got to their feet, too. Teenage kids who'd been sitting on the grass behind the benches and off to the sides also leapt to their feet, and those folks who'd already been standing, stood a little taller.

And clapped.

Brother, did they clap.

Everyone was standing and applauding, and though Hopp hadn't realized it at the time, when those sirens goosed him off that bench, he was leading a standing ovation.

And so Hopp and Elam and me, we just stood there and clapped till our hands got red, not knowing why the hell we were clapping, but when you're in the front row and a standing ovation is going on, you don't ask questions: you just stand and clap and grin like everybody else.

Over in the street, in front of the concession wagons and Highway Patrol car, in front of the stolen Mustang and the bank, in an open place vacated by the high school band members who had disappeared somewhere, two more Highway Patrol cars slid up and stopped, and behind them came a long black Cadillac, the sort of car you see in a funeral procession or gangster movie.

The high school band reappeared, bringing up the rear of the black Cadillac. They were marching and playing "On Wisconsin."

(No, I do not know why a high school band in Wynning, Iowa, would be playing "On Wisconsin." Why don't you ask the Chinese lady in the Tacomobile?)

And then the black car came to a stop, too, and the Highway Patrolmen were out of their cars and swarming all over everywhere. I never saw so many Highway Patrolmen in my life. I have to admit, thinking back, I can only count six of them, but at the time it seemed like there was a Highway Patrolman for every citizen in that park.

A little man in a well-tailored conservative brown suit, with a nicely chosen yellow-and-white pattern tie, followed a pair of Highway Patrolmen from the black Cadillac to the stage. The pair of Highway Patrolmen cleared an imaginary path for him through a non-existent throng: the Wynning citizens were clapping wildly, but were a mild-mannered, mini-mob who stayed in their places while whoever this was made his grand entrance.

Soon the little man, who had short brown hair and was about forty and handsome in an ordinary sort of way, was standing on the stage, near the microphone.

When the applause finally began to dwindle, one of the five men who'd already been on the stage—a pudgy, jolly-looking bald man with glasses—spoke into the mike. "It is with great pride and pleasure that the people of Wynning welcome to this, our 100th Founder's Day Celebration, our esteemed and honorable . . ."

(And this was shouted into the microphone)

". . . Governor of the State of Iowa!"

I thought I could hear Elam moaning, but it was hard to tell as the applause again began to swell.

As the ovation continued, Hopp leaned across me to ask Elam, "What now, smartass?"

"We just gotta stick it out," Elam said, leaning across me to answer Hopp. "We'll just stay here and listen to what this jerk has to say. He won't stay all day."

"I hope *we* don't," I said.

"We're okay as long as that goofy buddy of yours stays put," Elam told me. "He won't panic, will he? He'll just wait out there till we can join him, right? I mean, if he drives in here, man, the way they got roads blocked off and cars parked in the streets, we could get stuck here till the cows come home."

I didn't answer.

Because I had already spotted a tall, awkward-looking apparition walking along the perimeter of the park, looking confused, searching for a familiar face in the sea of standing, clapping bodies. And he was grinning like a rabbit, coming toward us now.

"Hey you guys," he said, joining in with the continuing applause, "what's goin' on? Is that *really* the Governor? I bet my mom'd get a kick out of this."

One good thing about being stuck there in the first row with all those people behind us and the Governor up on stage in front of us was that otherwise Wheaty probably would be dead right now. Because there was a moment when Elam and/or Hopp would have killed him, I think, if there hadn't been so many witnesses. And maybe I would have, too. If his mom wanted some of the action, she'd have to stand in line.

Wheat was oblivious to the danger, of course. He still thought the robbery was only a trial run, and had just gotten bored out there waiting for us. Not scared, you heard me right the first time: bored. According to Elam's plan of action, we should have reported back to that farmhouse within twenty-five minutes of leaving it. When an hour had passed, Wheat drove in to find out what was happening.

"What about the car?" Elam whispered, over the applause for the Governor, which was just beginning to dwindle.

"It's parked back here," Wheat said, and jerked a thumb over his shoulder, as he squeezed in between Hopp and me.

Back beyond the crowd we could see cars parked bumper to bumper in the street behind the park.

That was the moment when Elam and/or Hopp (and maybe me) almost killed Wheat.

But the only thing that died at that moment was the applause, and suddenly everybody was sitting down and we were all listening to the Governor.

Sort of.

I mean, I can't tell you what the Governor of the state of Iowa said that morning. It was a short speech, probably a lot like all the other pleasant, meaningless speeches you hear governors make in public, whether it's at a Fourth of July picnic or the opening of a new supermarket.

There were some reporters taking pictures. Three of them. They wore shiny plastic badges that said where they were from, and had camera equipment in leather packing, slung over their shoulders like purses. One of them was from the *Des Moines Register*, another from the *Daily Iowan* of Iowa City, and one from the *Port City Journal*. All of them were young and had longish hair and were casually dressed; tomorrow's Pulitzer Prize winners, starting at the bottom. At one time or another during the Governor's speech, each of the three reporters was crouched directly in front of us. When they took a picture, there was a whirring sound from the camera vaguely reminiscent of somebody cocking a gun.

The presence of the reporters, and the sound their cameras made, made me uneasy. I began to squirm. Elam gave me a sharp look to let me know my uneasiness was showing, and to cut it out. Both Elam and Hopp did terrific jobs of acting inconspicuous and unconcerned. Elam, especially. Hopp just sort of sat there like a stone, the way he did when he was playing cards; but Elam looked like he really felt at home, and even managed to chuckle when something was supposed to be funny.

Wheaty also seemed to be enjoying himself. That same capacity that made him able to enjoy his stay in jail was allowing him to find fascination in these cornball Founder's Day proceedings.

And those proceedings did have a certain fascination to them I must admit.

For example, when the Governor's speech was over, the Mayor presented him with the key to the city. It was a small key, like the trunk key to a Toyota. Considering the size of Wynning, that only seemed fitting.

Then after the Governor sat down, the Mayor gave a stirring recounting of the history of Wynning. It seems one hundred years ago a man named Wynning and his family settled here. A town grew up. Every year a Founder's Day Celebration had been held. This was the 100th such celebration. Thank you.

Wild applause followed the Mayor's oration. It was like the Gettysburg Address had been spoken for the first time. The reason for the enthusiasm was clearly the Governor. Never before had a Governor attended the yearly celebration. A new page was being written into the history of Wynning. I could hardly wait for next year's speech.

The Mayor stayed on his feet for the duration of the program. There were two reasons for this. One reason was that the Mayor was the emcee. The other was that now that the Governor had sat down, there weren't any chairs left.

Wheaty liked the next part a lot. The Wynning Founder's Day Queen and her court were presented. Evidently the crowning of the Queen at the beauty pageant of some sort had been held the night before. It was hard to believe a town so small could have enough good-looking young girls to populate a beauty pageant. It was harder still to believe when the girls appeared.

There were five of them, five apparent girls in bright summery dresses that seemed to have been ordered from a ten-year-old Ward's catalog. The girls climbed awkwardly onto the stage (there were not steps up to the bandshell from the ground) and displayed thighs of varying quality.

Three of the girls were, in fact, spectacularly homely. The sun bounced off braces on most of the female teeth on that stage. Two of the girls were sisters, it seemed safe to assume, as they shared the same stark red hair and freckles, although the freckles may have been acne, I never got close enough to check; each sister did, however, have her own individual, distinctive homeliness. The other homely girl who was not a redhead or a sister of the redheaded girls either, except perhaps in spirit, had apparently entered the beauty contest in hopes first prize was a nose job. The other two girls were not homely. One was skinny and plain, but a raving beauty in comparison to the sister act and the girl with the nose. The other girl was a lovely, shapely brunette, with a heart-shaped face, large, luminous brown eyes and a dainty nose; her cheeks were flushed with excitement (for, after all, she was the one who'd been crowned Queen of Wynning Founder's Day) and her teeth were straight and white and braceless. She had three inescapable physical characteristics, which can best be described by the following approximate figures: 38 D, and six foot two.

I heard somebody breathing hard.

It was Wheat.

His eyes were popping and his mouth was open.

He was in love.

"Kitch," he said. "I'm in love."

"One of the redheads, right?" I whispered.

"No! The big one! The tall girl with the long hair and the long legs and the big boobies!"

Elam said, "Shut up you two."

After the applause trailed off, the girls began introducing themselves, giving brief personal histories that must not have come as great surprise to the assembled residents of their Toyota trunk of a hometown.

Each girl was a recent high school graduate planning to attend one of the nearby community colleges or the University of Iowa. The two redheads were planning to major in home economics. The girl with the nose was going into pre-med. The skinny, plain girl was an English Lit major and wanted to be a poet.

The Queen was a phys ed major.

The Mayor played Bert Parks and asked the Queen, who was dressed virginal white with a rhinestone tiara in her long brown hair, how she felt about her honor.

She said "I am thrilled from head to toe," which in her case was quite a distance.

Then there was more applause and the Queen and her court climbed back down off the stage, showing thigh again, especially the Queen, who had quite a lot of it to show.

Wheat followed the Queen as she disappeared into the crowd. Followed her with his eyes, that is. Hopp was holding onto Wheat by the elbow, not about to let him get out of sight. Wheat was used to Hopp being somewhat irritable and thought nothing of it. I wondered if there was some way of keeping the truth away from Wheat. Telling him about the bank robbery (which was, technically, still in progress) was apt to set him off. A few minutes ago, before Wheat had showed up, Elam had asked if I thought Wheat capable of panic. I hadn't had the chance to answer him, but soon Elam should find out first-hand just how foolish that question had been.

Only the more I thought about it, the more it seemed a bad idea to tell Wheaty about the robbery. And as the program on the bandshell stage drew to a close, I whispered that opinion to Elam. "Listen, he'll freak. He really will. Take my word for it. Let's leave well enough alone."

Elam whispered back, "What do you suggest we tell him, them?"

"Nothing."

"Nothing?"

"Nothing except we're not happy he parked his car where he did, making us stuck here in the middle of the trial run."

Elam nodded.

"And," I continued, "he'll understand that naturally we don't want to attract much attention, since we're in town getting ready for the real thing."

Elam nodded some more. "You're a smart kid," he said, with his sinister smile. "Ha! Maybe I oughta cut you in on the take."

I swallowed hard. "I'll pass on that, thanks."

"Hey you guys," Wheat said. "Quiet. This is interesting."

The Mayor was telling about the forthcoming events of the day. There was to be entertainment, much of it there on the bandshell stage: an amateur-hour type contest; a concert by a female glee club from West Liberty; and a reprise of the talent numbers the girls in the Wynning Founder's Day Queen contest had performed the night before. The big tent was for a marathon bingo game, "only a 25-cent donation per card, and lots of big prizes." The Grange Hall, which was on the side street Wheat's car was parked in, was the scene of an antique show, a needlepoint and ceramics display, and a fine arts competition. Hot meals could be had, for a pittance, at the VFW Hall;

and the local tavern had been transformed into a beer garden, for today only, with mugs of beer for a nickel and pitchers for fifty cents. In between the various entertainment presentations on the bandshell stage, there was also to be dancing in the streets. Or more specifically, dancing in the street, you guessed it, the street the stolen Mustang was parked along. There was to be square dancing, and then a country western band would play, after which there'd be a teen dance. It was beginning to look like a long day.

At this point the Mayor concluded his remarks, thanked the Governor for coming and everybody stood and clapped again, and the program was over. People rushed forward to meet the Governor, shake his hand, get his autograph, and we quietly rose from our front-row seats and gathered under a tree at the rear of the park, away from any Wynning citizens.

Elam took immediate command. He had apparently whispered to Hopp the game plan about leaving Wheat in the dark, and merely said, calmly, "Okay. So we're stuck here for the day, looks like. Unless you can move that car of yours, Wheat, without making a thousand other people move their cars too. No? Okay. Then we got to blend in. Be part of Flounder's Day, hey hey. Enjoy ourselves."

"How?" I asked.

Wheaty said, "Let's all go drink nickel beer."

Elam said, "No. Getting crocked ain't exactly a good way of stayin' on top of things. No, much as I'd like it, the beer garden is out. Besides, we should split up. Bein' strangers in town on a day like this is bad to begin with. Bein' a group of strangers stickin' to each other like fly paper's worse yet. So we each go a separate way. Now. Who wants to do what?"

Hopp said, "I'll play bingo."

"Hopp's got bingo," Elam said. He turned to Wheat. "What about you?"

"I'll drink nickel beer," Wheat said.

Elam said, with incredible patience, "You'll go to the antiques show and that other junk at the, what is it?"

"Grange Hall," I said.

"Grange Hall," Elam said. "Understand?" And he prodded Wheat's chest, gently, with a stiff finger.

Wheat said he understood. Then he said, "My mom collects antiques."

Everybody looked at him for a moment, trying to figure out what that had to do with anything, and when nobody could, Elam finally went on, turning to me and saying, "You. You plop your butt on one of them benches over there and just watch the entertainment. And watch everything else, too. Keep an eye on what's goin' on, and if the situation changes at all, come tell us, *each* of us. For example, if those cops move their car for some reason, givin' us a berth to get out. Or if, uh, the situation should change in any other way, if you know what I mean, kid."

I knew what he meant. He meant watch the bank.

"Now," Elam said, thoughtfully, "all I got to do is figure out something for myself."

"Excuse me," the Mayor said.

He was on the stage. Talking in the mike.

"Excuse me" he said again, "but we seem to be missing someone. Has anyone seen Jack Wynning?"

There was no particular response from the audience. (And in case you're wondering, a lot of people in Wynning were named Wynning. I didn't find that out till later, but I don't see any reason not to tell you now.)

The Mayor repeated his question and then added, jokingly, "I hope our local banker hasn't run off with all our money." Some of the crowd laughed.

Elam, Hopp and I were not among the amused.

"Hey," Elam said. "He's talking about that damn banker."

Wheaty didn't catch the full significance of that, of course, not realizing that the banker in question was bound and gagged in the bank across the street.

Someone from down in the audience was handing a note up to the Mayor.

"Oh," he said, "Jack's daughter says her father was called out of town on business, at the last minute."

Elam grinned.

So did Hopp.

So did I.

Wheat said, "What are you guys grinning about?"

"I'm afraid," the Mayor was saying, "that Jack's absence presents a problem. We're now one cook short over at the VFW Hall. Anyone who'd like to volunteer, please come forward. Is there a short order cook in the house?"

"See ya later," Elam said, and went forward.

After Hopp headed off for the bingo tent, I took Wheat by the arm and said, "Don't screw around."

"What do you mean, Kitch?"

"This is a serious thing. These guys have us involved in a serious thing."

"Who says they don't?"

"Wheat, did you like jail?"

"It wasn't a bad place to visit, but I wouldn't want to live there."

"Well keep that in mind, because if you take this too lightly, we just might be living there for a while."

"I understand that, Kitch."

"Good. Now run along and be inconspicuous."

"No problem," he said, and wandered off.

I myself went and found a bench (not in the front row, this time!) and sat, entertaining not just a few doubts about Wheat's ability to be inconspicuous.

No entertainment was as yet under way on the bandshell stage. The Governor was still standing down in front of the bandshell, chatting with his constituents, granting autographs, while Highway Patrolmen lurked in the backgorund. This went on for another fifteen minutes or so, and finally the Governor departed, waving as he walked back to his black Cadillac. Soon the Cadillac and the two accompanying Highway Patrol vehicles had managed U-turns in the relatively narrow Wynning main street and were headed out of town.

This left the street temporarily clear, though the Mustang was still banked (you should pardon the expression) by the remaining Highway Patrol car and the Tacomobile. Still, the departure of the other Patrol cars was good news indeed. I considered asking the Chinese lady in the Tacomobile if she could back up just a hair, so we could get our car out. Those other two Highway Patrolmen were apparently here for the day, but presently they seemed to be swallowed up in the crowd, and the crowd itself's attention was hardly drawn toward the bank, so perhaps the money could be moved from the bank to the car without anyone noticing. It was still risky, to say the least, but I began to wonder if we'd been hasty in settling down for the Founder's Day duration. Maybe we would be able to get out of Wynning, yet. In one piece, even.

I was just getting up off the bench, to go tell everybody about the Governor and the Highway Patrol cars leaving, and about my idea for us leaving too, when the trucks rolled in.

Platform trucks. Two of them. The type of truck that has a sort of floor it drags along behind its cab, just a flat open floor. A platform.

The two trucks took up a lot of the space in the street.

Both of them pulled down by the saw-horse divider that was blocking the street off, and as soon as they had come to a stop, two panel trucks rolled in and joined them.

The panel trucks had writing on them. One had the words "Country Plowboys" written on the side. One had the word "Rox" written on the side. I watched, in fascination and horror, as amplifiers and other sound equipment was hauled out of the panel trucks and set up on the platforms of the platform trucks. It was, of course, the country western band (the Plowboys) and the rock group (Rox) who were setting up to play dance music at different intervals during the afternoon and perhaps (I shuddered to think) the evening, as well.

Meanwhile, the talent show was getting under way on the stage. A boy of about thirteen was playing "Jesus Christ Superstar" on a saw. What can I say.

After the musical saw number terminated, a girl played a medley of Beatles songs on the Hammond organ, which gave me the insane urge to rollerskate to Liverpool, and I began looking at people in the crowd, studying them, trying to see who made up the little town of Wynning.

They were just people. Not hicks, either. There was a certain number of men who were obviously farmers, with old-fashioned apparel of the man who works on a farm and is proud of it. But the wives and children of these men didn't look any different from the wives and children of the middle class anywhere.

Of course I admit I grew up in Nebraska, and went to school in Illinois, and that naturally means the ways of the Middle West aren't new to me. They are, in fact, all I know. But as far as I can tell, those ways aren't particularly different from any place else in the country. Television is probably what's done it, what's made us all pretty much the same. I guess maybe we should be thankful for things like the Wynning Founder's Day, and other regional nonsense, designed to make us remember we come from towns and states, and not just a country.

Anyway, the people here looked normal enough. The town seemed to have its share of kids with long hair and fashionably sloppy clothes, and pretty young girls in stylish, sexy outfits, and young married couples wearing the same sort of clothes young married couples in New York wear on a hot summer day, I suppose. And little kids were running around and making noise and falling down and wearing clothes that were already dirty, even though the morning was barely half over.

I also thought I could pick out a few University people. Wynning is just a stone's toss from Iowa City and the University of Iowa, and apartments and houses in a university town are hard (and expensive) to come by, so not surprisingly a certain number of bearded, pipe-smoking men in poorly fitting somber sportshirts walked arm in arm with lean-faced, short-haired liberated women wearing studiously unattractive slacks and sweaters.

One person, though, particularly caught my eye. This person was female, as you may have guessed. This person was wearing a red, white and blue sparkle swim suit.

Well, not exactly a swim suit, but that's as close as I can come to describing it properly. You see, she was the band majorette I mentioned before, briefly, and she was really something. She had blond hair and dark blue eyes. She had a very nice figure. She looked familiar to me, but then all pretty girls look somewhat familiar; I mean, the conventional sort of attributes that make girls pretty makes for a lot of them looking alike. If you follow me.

I followed her, with my eyes, as she practiced with her baton, out in the street; she had the good sense not to bother with the entertainment on the bandshell stage (right now a middle-aged heavy-set lady was imitating Groucho Marx) and was prancing out there, probably playing the exhibitionist more than practicing her baton work (which was as flawless as it was intricate) and had drawn a crowd of guys, who were watching, with round-eyed adoration.

The more I watched her, the more familiar she looked. Wishful thinking you might say, but I really felt I had seen her somewhere before, though what any acquaintance of mine would be doing in Wynning was beyond me, too, so I kept studying her, forcing myself to focus on her face, to try to dredge up the memory of where it was I'd seen her before.

And then it came to me.

It was the girl I had bumped into when I was streaking through the DeKalb Holiday Inn. The girl in the bikini. There was no mistaking that young, pretty face. That blond hair. Those dark blue eyes. Or the rest of her, either.

And here I was staring at her! What if she noticed me, and, Lord! What if she recognized me, too?

As the thought passed through my mind that I had to turn away, before our eyes met, our eyes met. She dropped her baton.

She smiled.

She recognized me.

She rushed over, a blur of blond hair and flashing thighs and patriotic glitter, and said, "Well, hello!"

"Er," I said.

"What are you doing here?"

She giggled and scooted in next to me on the bench. "I almost didn't recognize you with your clothes on."

That elicited a startled look from the middle-aged couple on the other side of me, but my pretty majorette didn't seem to notice, or anyway care, and she bubbled on, "I'm so glad to see you! And surprised!"

A fat man in front of us turned and held a finger to pudgy lips and shushed us. There was a talent show going on, after all. A man was on stage doing tricks with a yo-yo.

"We better get out of here if we want to talk," she said. "Tell you what. I'll let you buy me a lemonade."

And before I could answer, she was standing up, and two of the nicest boobies (as Wheat would say) ever to be decorated in red, white and blue sparkles were looking right at me. She took my hand, pulled me to my feet and led me away.

Normally, I wouldn't mind at all being led away by a girl as beautiful as this, a girl who had that golden-haired wholesome look used in television commercials to make the American male think of sex and buy milk.

But I was in no mood for sex or milk or lemonade, either. I was, remember, in the middle of the worst situation of my life, and this vision of blond Midwestern liveliness was walking in at a most inopportune moment. I don't mean to be a complainer, but I think you'd have to agree that Fate just hadn't been on my side through this whole thing, and this was a hell of a time to throw me a crumb, even a beautiful, shapely crumb like this.

Anyway, pretty soon we were standing in front of the Tacomobile and she was saying, "You still haven't told me what you're doing in Wynning."

I opened my mouth, but my mind couldn't seem to find anything to fill the opening.

"I know!" she said, suddenly brightening. "You came to see *me*, didn't you!"

"Right," I agreed. "Right. To see you."

"How did you know where to look for me? How did you find me?"

"Uh," I said.

"You're a sly one," she said, nudging me in the ribs, winking. "Going to keep me guessing, huh?"

"If I, uh, told you how I found you," I heard myself saying, "that'd take, uh, some of the fun out of it. Some of the mystery."

A nice-looking brown-haired girl in one of the hideous marching band uniforms was ahead of us in line at the Tacomobile window. She heard us talking and turned and looked with envy and even scorn at her fellow band member wearing the skimpy, sparkly majorette outfit, and said, "Who's the new boyfriend, Sue Ann? Find a replacement for Bo Bo so soon?"

Sue Ann put her hands on her very attractive hips and smiled at her catty friend in genial defiance. "His name is Fred Kitchen," she said. "And he came all the way from Sycamore, Illinois, to see me, didn't you, Fred? Fred? Are you all right, Fred?"

I was Fred, all right. The TILT light in my head was going on, but I was Fred. I conjured up a smile as weak as my knees. "I'm fine," someone said. Me, apparently.

The brown-haired girl said, "Hi, Fred. I'm Julie." She extended a hand.

I looked at it. After a while I remembered about shaking hands, yes, that's a native American custom, shaking hands. I shook her hand. I shook period.

Sue Ann said, "Fred, are you sure you're all right? You look kind of sick."

"Uh, Sue Ann," I said. "Could we go someplace private and talk?"

The brown-haired girl, Julie, said, "Well!" huffily, like Jack Benny, and turned quickly away. I guess I hurt her feelings or offended her or something, although I hadn't meant to be rude; my mind was not organized enough at the moment for me to do anything so controlled as to be purposely rude to someone.

But Sue Ann didn't seem to mind my accidental rudeness, and even smiled at me for it. Even in my shell-shocked state, it was coming through that the two girls didn't like each other much.

So I bought lemonades at the Tacomobile window and Sue Ann led me behind the concession wagons up onto the step-up sidewalk, where we sat on the slight porch of one of the storefronts.

Sue Ann slurped at her lemonade. Through a straw. She had on some sort of pale, frosty lipstick that made her lips glisten like the sparkles on her skimpy suit.

So she knew me. I remembered vaguely telling here my name was Fred, when I bumped into her, streaking; but I didn't remember telling her Fred Kitchen. Or had I?

Finally she looked up from her lemonade and said, "Are you always so quiet, Fred?"

"No. I'm just a little . . . surprised."

"Surprised? Why? I'm the one who's surprised, having you come look me up like this!"

"Well, I'm surprised you remembered my name, is all."

"Silly! You were in all the papers! Don't you think I was interested, having bumped into you like I did? I almost felt famous myself! I saved all the clippings."

"No kidding?"

"Sure! That's a really funny picture, you know, of you and your friend streaking through those wedding guests. But maybe it doesn't seem so funny to you. I mean, going to jail and all."

"Jail wasn't so bad."

"Really? Well, I suppose if you're stuck inside a place like that for a whole month you learn to live with it. Maybe even make some friends, I suppose."

"I made some friends I'll never forget."

"I'll bet! Do you keep in touch with any of them?"

"Now and then."

She slurped her lemonade thoughtfully for a moment, then said, "Listen, Fred, I'm . . . I'm really touched by what you've done." I was touched, too: she was touching my knee. "I mean, it's really something, you going to so much trouble to track me down so you could see me again."

"It was nothing," I said.

"Hey," she said, "you know, it's not necessary for me to hang around here, at this Founder's Day thing. I mean, I'm done for the day. All I had to do was my majorette stuff when we marched in behind the governor's car, and that's it. I don't have any part in the band concert, later on, there's no part for a majorette in that, so . . . so how would you like to go over to my house, and try to think of something to do?"

I would like that fine. It was escape. Limited escape, perhaps. Illusionary, temporary escape, certainly. But escape.

Out of this Founder's Day nightmare, for a while at least.

"What . . . what if your parents should come home?" I asked.

"Who says we'd be doing anything they wouldn't approve of?" she asked, coyly. Then squeezed my knee again and said, "Besides, Mom's out of town, tending her sick sister. And Dad was called out of town, too, on business, unexpectedly."

"Your dad was what?"

"Called out of town on business, unexpectedly. He works right here." And she jerked a thumb over her shoulder at the building behind us.

At which point I realized for the first time we were sitting on the stoop in front of the bank.

When my heart started up again, I said, "Your . . . your father is the local banker?"

She nodded. "But don't you worry about him coming home. He's going to be tied up all day."

We walked to where she lived. It wasn't far. In fact it was just around the corner from the bank, on a street as quiet, clean and residential as those I'd driven through coming into town this morning. These homes were newer, however, and there were fewer trees. Modern houses, ranch styles mostly, three-bedroom numbers, sitting on flat, well-tended lawns. Wynning's two-and-a-half block housing addition.

Sue Ann Wynning, her mother and-father (Sue Ann was an only child, I quickly learned) lived in one of the nicest of these homes, a split level, with barnwood siding, a double garage and money written all over it.

"That's some house," I said, slightly awestruck, as

we walked up the driveway toward it.

We were arm in arm. Sue Ann was snuggling in against me. Affectionate child. She said, "It's okay. I liked our other house better."

"Other house?"

"Daddy wanted something smaller, this time."

"Smaller?"

We were walking up the front steps, now.

"Our other house, in Cedar Rapids, was one of those big old gothic places, with secret passages and a tower and everything. It was an estate, really."

"No kidding?"

Sue Ann opened the front door. It was unlocked. She said, "See, Daddy's sort of semi-retired. His family's been in banking for years, and he used to be president of the big bank in Cedar Rapids, like his Daddy before him."

"Is he old enough to be semi-retired?"

"Not really, but what with his heart condition and all, he doesn't have much choice."

"Heart condition?"

"Yes. He had a lot of stress in his work in Cedar Rapids, and the doctor told him to slow down, so he quit his president job and took this little branch office thing here in Wynning, four years ago."

"How . . . how bad is his heart condition?"

"Why, Fred! You seem really upset. I think you're trembling! What's the matter?"

"Uh, it's just, uh, there's been some heart trouble in my family, too, and it's something you really have to watch."

And then she looked at me like she had never seen such compassion before, like I was a saint. "Fred, I feel like I've known you for years," she said, breathlessly. Lips moist. Eyes hooded. "I feel I want to know you for years."

I wondered how she'd feel if she knew she was entertaining Charles Manson, which is who I might as well have been. It would make a good headline for the cheap tabloids: SHE FELL IN LOVE WITH HER FATHER'S MURDERER! I pictured myself walking down that long corridor to the little room where the electric chair would be waiting, my Methodist minister father walking alongside me, Bible in his hands, asking me why I took off my clothes and streaked through the DeKalb Holiday Inn.

"How about a tour?" she asked.

"Tour?"

"Of the house, silly. Fred, you don't take drugs, do you?"

"Uh, no. Of course not."

"Because I'm a firm believer in maintaining a healthy body."

"I can see that."

"And well, I couldn't go for a boy who took drugs. I like a good time like anybody else, but I'm anti-drug as heck."

"Me too."

"Then how come you look so strung out?"

"Oh. Do I? Well. I'm just, uh . . ."

"I know," she said with a Mona Lisa smile. "I understand. Really I do."

I was glad *somebody* did.

"You're surprised," she continued, coming over and sitting in my lap.

"I . . . I sure am."

"I mean you're surprised to find that I feel the same way about you as you do about me. You met me just for a moment, and yet I stayed in your thoughts. No, now don't be shy. Don't be modest. That's how it was. Just like in the song."

"The song?"

"'Some Enchanted Evening'."

She sang a few bars. She was a soprano.

"We did *South Pacific* in high school," she explained. "I had the lead."

"You really ought to go out for Founder's Day Queen. You'd be a snap to win talent."

"Don't be so silly. That rinky-dink thing! Did you see that bunch of dogs they had this year? It's a joke. Besides, I couldn't be in it because I was already committed to be band majorette."

"I see."

"Where was I, Fred?"

"You were singing 'Some Enchanted Evening' in my lap."

"Oh. Yes. Anyway, you saw me for just a moment, but that moment meant something to you. You remembered me. You came looking for me, like a detective or something. And you didn't know it, but

I felt the same way about you. Especially when I saw that picture of you in all the papers and everything. Did you know you were on the NBC news?"

"No I didn't."

"John Chancellor told about you streaking, and that you got thirty days for it. He smiled when he told about the streaking, and frowned when he told about the thirty days."

"No kidding?"

"Now do you see why I felt famous just bumping into you that fateful night?" And she grinned and giggled after saying the phrase "fateful night" and then leaned up and gave me a big, wet, soulful kiss.

And hot. I left that out: hot. Maybe that was implied in soulful, but I want to get across to you just how powerful a kisser this girl was. She really put herself into it, and I appreciated the effort.

She kissed me a few more times, and when she was done, she said, "How about it?"

"How . . . how about what?" I said, drunkenly. Hopefully.

"How about that tour I promised you?" she said, hopping out of my lap, giving me a teasing grin, and then taking me by the hand again, hauling me out of the chair and leading me around the house.

I could tell her family had indeed lived in a bigger, older home at one time, as the place was filled to overflowing with early American antiques. With the open-beam wood ceilings and all, the antiques looked great, and I would have moved into that house in a second. It was the sort of home I might have one day owned myself, if I hadn't gotten into this mess.

The house had a strongly masculine look to it, with wood dominating both in the open ceilings and paneled walls. Even the master bedroom shared by man and wife had a dark, manly look to it. But the final room she took me to was so different in appearance it almost belonged in another house.

The only wood in the room was the open-beam ceiling, and the sliding doors of the closet, and this wood was that same dark masculine stuff prevalent through the rest of the house. But there was no wood paneling in here. In its place was ultra-feminine blue and white flowery wallpaper, with dark blue curtains on the windows and a matching blue, ruffly-skirted bedspread. The blue in the room was approximately the same color as Sue Ann's eyes. The furniture was antiqued white wood: a dresser with oversize mirror; a chest of drawers; and a canopy bed. Double bed. The floor was carpeted in fluffy stuff that looked like whipped egg whites. It was a large room, as large as the master bedroom; an only child's room. Very tidy, almost fussily so, except for a big bulletin board on one wall, haphazardly covered with withered corsages, buttons with funny sayings and/or school-related club names, and a lot of photographs of Sue Ann, as a cheerleader, majorette and in school plays, several apparently from that high school production of *South Pacific* she'd mentioned.

"This is your bedroom," I said. (I catch onto things

quick, as you may have noticed.)

"I said I saved the best for last, silly," she said. She turned around. "Unsnap me."

"Unwhat you?"

"Unsnap me. And then unzip me, too."

She shimmied out of the sparkly majorette uniform. It lay in a patriotic puddle at her feet. She was wearing sheer panties under the uniform, but not for long.

She stood with her hands on her hips and let me take a long, lustful look at a perfect young female body, which she apparently was very proud of. And rightly so. Her skin was pale, but in a healthy way, and she was lean and shapely and smooth looking.

"Now don't get any ideas," she said.

I stood there for a moment and thought about what to make of a girl who takes off her clothes and says don't get any ideas.

"I just thought that since I saw you naked, you ought to get to see me naked."

"That seems fair."

"But I think we ought to get to know each other a little better before it goes any farther than just looking. Don't you, Fred?"

"I'm enjoying just looking. I'll settle for looking."

She came up and pressed herself against me and put her arms around my neck and gave me a kiss that would've melted a statue.

"Well," she said, nibbling my ear, "I guess we could sort of get in bed and just neck a little. That wouldn't hurt. But nothing else. Just neck a little."

"That would be nice," I said.

"Why don't you just go ahead and take your clothes off, too. I think that would make the necking more pleasant, don't you? But we'll have to be good."

"I think we could be good," I said.

"At least," she agreed.

I took off my clothes.

She got in bed and so did I and we necked. Nothing else. Just necked.

And if you buy that, I got some jewelry in the car to show you.

I was not supposed to be in Sue Ann's bed. I was supposed to be sitting on a bench in the park, watching things, the bank in particular.

But I was glad I was in Sue Ann's bed, and not just for the obvious reasons, either. I was glad to get Sue Ann away from that crowded park, where she would be likely to introduce me to more and more of her friends, where eventually the streaking bit was bound to come up, in which case I could find myself all of a sudden a minor celebrity. The center of attention. Which clearly wouldn't do.

Furthermore, I had no choice but to follow Sue Ann wherever she might choose to lead me (even into bed) because my presence in Wynning was explainable to her only by my being there to see her. So what else could I do but see her?

The unpleasant coincidence of her father being the local banker seemed somewhat irrelevant, as far as the immediate situation was concerned. It had its good side in that Sue Ann and I were guaranteed privacy in their house; but it also had its bad side, as eventually Sue Ann might discover the real purpose for my presence in Wynning, and her opinion of me would probably change.

At any rate, there was nothing I could do about being stuck in Sue Ann's bed except enjoy myself. I even began to think everything might work out for the good, should Elam and Hopp get themselves caught and have the courtesy not to implicate Wheat and me. After all, I had an excuse for being here. Sue Ann. And Wheat had an excuse for being here, too: he was my friend, and along for the ride.

So I began to loosen up a little, put the worrying aside for a while, though the credit for that had to go to Sue Ann. I whole-heartedly recommend a few hours in bed with a beautiful girl to any guy caught up in a hopeless mess. It's a terrific way to get your mind off your problems.

After that first hour in bed, Sue Ann asked me if I'd like some lunch.

Cotton candy was all I'd had to eat today, and since I seemed to have worked up an appetite somehow or other, I accepted her offer and we went down to the kitchen where Sue Ann made a submarine sandwich, a huge one stuffed with cheese and salami and lettuce and tomatoes and sweet peppers, and we shared it.

Sue Ann was sitting across the table from me, nibbling at her sandwich, wearing a baby blue terrycloth robe (I was in a similar, white robe—her father's—and I admit I didn't feel particularly comfortable wearing it). In between nibbles, she'd ask me questions about myself. Was I still in college? What were my plans when I got out? Did I have any other, serious girl friend? Questions like that. It was pleasant answering such questions. Made me feel alive again. I asked her what her aspirations were. She wanted to be either an actress or a wife. If the latter, she'd like to be married to an actor or somebody else famous or rich or both. She'd been going with a Shaker Saltz type named Bo Bo Harper, a Little All-American football player, but they had broken up several weeks ago, and for good: he was heading off to Michigan State on a scholarship and wanted to "date around" but Sue Ann was all or nothing, monogamous or forget it, Bo Bo. Her immediate plans were college at the University of Iowa, since she had graduated from high school that June.

The conversation went on like that. Nothing spectacular. I remember every word of it, and could bore you with it if you insist. But why not just leave it this way: we were getting to know each other, in a backwards way I admit, since we'd just come down from her bedroom; but nevertheless getting to know each other is what we were doing.

The impression Sue Ann had given me, up till now, was that she was not terribly bright and was somewhat conceited. Now that I was getting to know her better, I found I'd been right.

I also found I liked her.

For one thing, she was beautiful. The Sue Ann Wynnings of the world have not generally invited me to their bedrooms so early in the game. Or late in the game, either, if you must know. So her being beautiful, and her willingness to share her beauty with me, had a lot to do with my forgiving her flaws.

That is, if you consider her being less than genius material a flaw. The dumb blonde stereotype has always been attractive to me, and if Sue Ann fit that stereotype a little, it only enhanced her beauty in my eyes. And besides, she was no dummy. She was an A- student in high school, she said (although with her looks even her grade average may have come easy) and I began to realize her dumb blonde appearance was at least partially an appealing affectation, made so by the naive, practically childlike side of her which gave her an aura of innocence even as she was inviting me under the covers with her.

That same quality of innocence took the edge off her conceit, too. She was pleased with her good looks, but not obnoxious about it.

Anyway, after lunch we went back to bed, and then after while I did something that was very, very stupid.

I fell asleep.

Voices woke me.

I sat up, startled. Startled to hear voices. Startled to find I'd fallen asleep.

It was dark in the room. That startled me, too. Where was the sunlight? This morning and afternoon, sunlight had filtered in through the semi-sheer curtains. Where was it now? I got out of bed, went to the window, parted the curtains. Darkness.

Also known as night.

Meanwhile, the voices were continuing. A male voice. And Sue Ann's voice. Seemed to be coming from the living room, which was down the hall, down a brief flight of steps to the lower part of the split level. I could make out no words. Just Sue Ann's voice and a male voice.

A low, rumbling, mature-sounding male voice. An older man's voice.

Damn!

Her father?

That couldn't be her father, could it?

I decided to put on my clothes.

I decided also to make the bed.

Then I went to the dresser and pulled the chair out and sat down and tried to think.

I had fallen asleep. Okay. An idiotic thing to do, but understandable. I'd had little or no sleep the night before. I'd spent the morning getting caught up in a situation that became ever more taxing with each turn of the screw.

So I had dozed off. But for how long?

A clock on Sue Ann's dresser answered my question: it was a quarter after eight.

Which meant I'd slept for around seven hours.

Seven hours! I felt numb at the thought. I felt like passing out, but I couldn't allow myself the luxury: it might be another seven hours before I came out of it!

I wondered what had happened while I was asleep.

I wondered what Wheat was up to. I wondered how Elam had made out as a fill-in cook. I wondered how well Hopp had managed to disappear into a bingo game that I assumed must've otherwise consisted of little old ladies.

I wondered if anyone had discovered the people tied up in the bank.

I wondered if one of those people belonged to the deep male voice talking to Sue Ann down in the bowels of the house.

I wondered if they let you play cards in prison.

Footsteps.

The door opened.

Sue Ann.

She was wearing a scoop-neck calico blue tee-shirt top, and snug-fitting blue jeans. She looked cute and sexy and a little tired.

She smiled and came over and gave me a kiss. Not a hot one this time. Just a hello kiss.

She said, "I see you're up and dressed. And you made the bed, too. I bet you heard me talking to Uncle Phil and got scared, didn't you! Don't be such a silly. Come on down and say hi."

"Do you, uh, think that's wise?"

"My uncle doesn't care what I do with my boy friends, silly. He's very hip. But, heck, you know that. I mean, you've met him before."

"I have?"

"He told me so, when I mentioned you were here. He seemed delighted. He's waiting downstairs to see you."

"Sue Ann, I have never met your uncle."

"Look, I've already figured out how you found out about me, if you're still trying to keep that a secret."

"I'm really not following this at all, Sue Ann."

"Hey, now, don't be mad at Uncle Phil for telling on you. He didn't say a word. I figured it out myself."

"You did?"

"Sure! When I found out you'd been to his house, I knew why you'd gone over there. I knew you looked Uncle Phil up so you could find out about me. So now I know, and you're afraid some of the romance has gone out of it, right? Don't be silly. And don't pout! I'd have made you tell me yourself, sooner or later."

"Really, Sue Ann, I . . ."

"Come on," she said, grabbing my hand and pulling me out of the chair. "He's waiting to say hi. Come on!"

I gave up. I offered absolutely no resistance, and let her lead me down the hall, down the steps, into the living room. Where a heavy-set man was rising off the sofa and extending a hand. He was not a good-looking man. He had a little head on his big body, a receding hairline, bulging eyes, wide mouth. He was wearing the same yellow shirt and tan shorts he'd been wearing the day I met him at his home.

"Well, well!" DeKalb 's Chief of Police said,

cheerfully. "If it isn't my little girl's favorite reception guest!"

There was no time to be surprised or shocked or anything. Besides, by this point I was pretty well used to having the worst happen. And I guessed this must be the worst yet.

"So you've taken a shine to my little niece, huh?" the Chief (or Uncle Phil, as Sue Ann thought of him) said. "Can't say as I blame you. Tell me, if you marry her, are you going to have the reception at the Holiday Inn?" And he laughed boisterously.

I laughed too, but I'm afraid mine was more along the lines of hysterical.

Neither Sue Ann nor her uncle caught that, however, and the Chief put a hand on my shoulder and said, "You look a little worried, son. I hope it's not because of me."

I said, "Well, uh . . ."

Sue Ann said, "Why should he be worried because of you, Uncle Phil?"

The Chief said, "I'm an officer of the law, honey, and he's afraid I might interfere with what he's doing here." My knees began to knock. Knees really can do that, you know.

Sue Ann said, "I don't get you, Uncle Phil."

"Kitchen here does," the Chief said, and winked at me, and punched my arm playfully. "But don't you worry, son. I don't have any jurisdiction here. I'm just another Wynning boy come home to roost for the big celebration. Sue Ann's dad and me are great-great nephews of the man who founded this little town. We never actually lived here, of course, but like a lot of people named Wynning scattered here and there around the countryside, we make a thing of getting here for the annual Founder's Day blowout. Sue Ann's dad always wanted to retire to here, and I guess he has at that. Anyway, frankly, I think what you're here for'll be great for the town. Terrific publicity, what with all the reporters around." And he narrowed his eyes conspiratorially and said, "Just don't get caught."

"Uh . . . uh, I'll do my best, sir," I said. I wasn't sure I was hearing this. Why on earth would the DeKalb Police Chief want to help me get away with robbing a bank? Was he crazy, or was it me? Or both of us? Or was I still sleeping up in Sue Ann's canopy bed?

He punched me on the arm again. I wasn't asleep. He grinned and said, "Well, I hate to run, but it's well after eight, and the big watermelon-eating contest is at eight-thirty, and I don't want to miss that. See you kids later. And Sue Ann?"

"Yes, Uncle Phil?"

"You give your daddy hell when he gets home tonight, for skipping out today. Isn't like him to miss Founder's Day. And I thought he was supposed to be taking it easy these days. What's he running around the countryside on business for, anyhow? The mercenary so-and-so."

Sue Ann said she'd relay that message, and her uncle pumped my hand, looked right at me and laughed like I was the funniest thing he'd ever seen, advised me again not to get caught, and left.

We sat on the couch. Sue Ann did not seem as puzzled as I was, so I asked her, "What was he talking about?"

"About not getting caught? What do you think? He knows you're here to see me. He knows we've been alone together all afternoon in the house. He probably means don't let my daddy catch you and me in my bedroom, silly. What else could he mean?"

"Oh, I don't know."

"He's a fantastic uncle. Really great. I mean, look at his attitude about when you streaked my cousin's wedding."

Cousin's wedding? Okay. Okay . . . now *Uncle* Phil the DeKalb Police Chief was making sense to me. I hadn't had the time to put it together before.

Sue Ann had been staying at the Holiday Inn in DeKalb because she was there for the wedding. That's what she'd been talking about earlier, when she said she knew how I figured out where she lived. She thought I had checked at the Holiday Inn to get her name, and that I'd found out she was the niece of the DeKalb Police Chief, and that I'd looked up the Chief to find out more about her.

"Tell me, Sue Ann," I said. "Why weren't you at the reception? Why were you in your swimming suit when I bumped into you?" Which of course was the reason why I hadn't thought of connecting her to the wedding.

"I'd already been there," she explained. "It was just a lot of old people, and boring relatives, and my cousin Kathy and her husband are older than I am too, so even the young guests were old. Clear into their twenties."

"I'm twenty-one, Sue Ann."

"But you don't seem that old, silly."

But I feel older, I thought. Much older.

"Anyway," she continued, "I got bored and left. So did Mom. We caught heck later, because we missed out on the family picture. Either way, I guess you and me would've run into each other, huh?"

"I guess so."

"Uncle Phil was tickled by all the publicity you got him by doing that at Kathy's reception. It saved him money on the wedding pictures."

"Yeah, he told me."

"Are you getting tired of hanging around here? You want to go back and do some of the Founder's Day stuff?"

"Maybe we should. Listen, I got to think for a few minutes. You suppose you could get me something to drink? A Coke or some ice tea or maybe some coffee?"

"Sure!"

She trotted off, and I sat and tried to put some more pieces together.

I doubted the Chief (Uncle Phil) had been talking about Sue Ann and me fooling around when he advised me not to get caught. But it was insanity to think he'd caught onto the robbery somehow and was not blowing the whistle because he liked me or thought it'd be good publicity for Wynning or something.

Then Sue Ann was handing me a glass of ice tea. I glanced up to thank her, and noticed she was naked.

When some girls take off their clothes, they just take off their clothes. When Sue Ann takes off her clothes, she's naked.

I forgot my problems for a second and smiled and reached out for her and she let out a giggle and ran off.

And I got an idea.

No, not the idea you think . . .

I found Elam sitting on the cement steps behind the Grange Hall. He was stripped down to his tee-shirt, with a dirty white apron around his waist and a battle-worn chef's hat on his head. He was smoking a cigarette and looked tired and, well, content. Lights were on in the kitchen behind him, where some guys were busily and somewhat noisily washing dishes.

"Long time no see," Elam said. "Have a seat."

"I see you've been keeping busy," I said, joining him on the steps.

"Keeping busy? Ha! Worked my butt off is what I did. Kid, I ain't worked so hard in years. Hell, I even made, what?" He stuck his hand in his pocket, took out some bills and some change. "Twenty-four dollars and forty cents."

"No kidding? How'd you manage that?"

"I told 'em I was just passin' through and had stopped to see what all the Founder's Day fuss was about, and heard the announcement they needed a cook, and I was one and'd be glad to do it. But since I wasn't a native citizen or anything, I felt I should get something for my trouble. They offered me two forty an hour and I grabbed it."

"You think it was smart, taking money from these people?"

"Would've been stupid not to. Ha! Why would a stranger offer to help out, otherwise? Just for the hell of it? Not damn likely. World ain't built that way, kid. But I got to admit I had a good time. That's a nice big kitchen to work in. Us short order jockeys usually get stuck in some closet with a griddle in it, and it's a kick workin' a nice big kitchen. People were okay, too. Not a bunch of hicks like I pictured."

"It's a nice little town."

"Yeah," Elam agreed, nodding. "Yeah, it is, isn't it?"

We sat there for a few moments, not saying anything, just enjoying the breeze that was skimming through the trees that stood in a row behind the Grange Hall, ruffling the leaves like a proud father playing with his kid's hair. I felt relaxed, almost comfortable.

I had dreaded coming to see Elam, even though I did have a way figured out to get out of town. Elam still frightened me, and parts of what I had to say to him might not go over too well. But right now, sitting here on the steps with him, enjoying the breeze, I didn't think it was going to be so bad.

Finally Elam finished his cigarette, arched it into the grass where it sizzled for what seemed like forever. The longer it sizzled, the less comfortable I felt.

"So," Elam said. "Where you been all day? I expected a progress report, now and then, you know."

"The Highway Patrol car is still parked in front of the Mustang," I said, "up against the bumper. The concession wagons are pulled in right behind. We're as trapped as we ever were."

"I see. Well, this Founder's Day isn't going to last all night."

"No. Just till around two o'clock this morning, is all."

Elam sighed. "Those lousy Highway Patrol guys must be getting paid overtime and then some. What are they doing at a thing like this, anyway? Why aren't they out patrolling the highway where they belong?"

"The County Sheriff's people are here, too," I said, "Haven't you seen those guys in the brown shirts and tan pants?"

"The guys that look like Forest Rangers or senile Boy Scouts or something? Yeah, I seen 'em. I didn't see any badges or guns on 'em, though."

"They don't have any. They're just a civilian volunteer outfit that helps out the Sheriff's department at functions like this. Sue Ann says the Highway Patrol isn't usually present for Founder's Day, but because this is the Centennial and the Governor came and the road's blocked off and everything, those two guys got assigned here."

"Who the hell is Sue Ann?"

"That's a long story."

"I been workin' in the kitchen all day, and you been foolin' with something called Sue Ann?"

"Well, if you want to make a long story short, yes."

"And I was telling you what a good time I had."

"You made twenty-four bucks, didn't you?"

"Yeah, and forty cents. So. Did you have anything else to tell me? Or did you just come around to say we're still stuck here?"

"I have something else to tell you."

"What, already?"

"I got a way figured out for us to get out of town."

"Good! Let's hear it."

"Okay," I said, and I told him my idea.

He laughed. Not derisively, either.

"That's beautiful kid," he said, tears in his eyes from laughing so hard. "You really got a mind for this kind of work. You sure you don't want a share of the loot? You deserve one, if anybody does."

"I'm sure," I said. "I'm, uh, sure of something else, too."

"What's that?" he asked, still laughing.

"You don't get a share, either. Or Hopp. Or Wheat, for that matter."

He stopped laughing.

"What?" he said. Clipped. Like a fast jab.

"I told you how we can get out of town. My idea is good. You agree with me. And I'm willing to go through with it. But the money is out. We have to leave it behind."

Elam looked at me for a long time. He didn't get mad. I thought he'd go absolutely off his nut, strangle me, jump up and down on me, everything. But I underestimated him. He was a professional. He knew I wouldn't suggest that if there wasn't a reason.

"Why?" he asked.

"Because otherwise Wheat and me won't get you out of this mess."

"Blackmail, huh?"

"There's more to it than that," I said, and told him. And, finally, reluctantly, he agreed.

"But don't tell Hopp," he said. "I'll tell him the money's already in the trunk, then break him the bad news later. He's a good man, but when he gets upset, he can cause a scene."

"Yeah," I nodded. "I got a friend like that, too."

Elam and I went to see Hopp, in the bingo tent.

There were four big long tables put together to form a square, and inside the square were four smaller tables covered with prizes. These tables also formed a square, and inside was a man with a microphone and a wire basket that whirled around, out of which he drew the numbers. The prizes ran mostly to small kitchen appliances, like toasters and mixers, many of them tagged and sort of set aside, which I assumed meant they'd already been won and would be collected by their winners at the end of the evening. The man with the microphone was hoarse and beginning to weave; evidently he'd been at this since the beginning, which was something like twelve hours ago. There were about a hundred people at the tables, mostly women, housewives and older ladies both, even a few teenagers and some old men. And Hopp.

Hopp sat between an old lady and housewife, both of whom were giving him plenty of room.

Hopp was playing eight cards.

Seeing him huddled over his cards, sitting there at the table, spine arched defiantly, brow knitted with concentration, took me back to the jail and the metal picnic tables where we'd played pitch and Hopp had said, "Deal the cards."

There was plenty of space for Elam and me to squeeze in on either side of him.

"Come on," Elam said.

Hopp stared down at his cards.

"B ten," said the man with the microphone.

"We're going," Elam said.

Hopp put a piece of corn on the upper left corner of the third card down from the right.

"We're leaving, I said," Elam said.

"Getting out of town," I said.

Hopp said, "Not yet."

"N forty," the man with the microphone said.

"Not yet?" Elam said.

"Not yet?" I said.

Hopp looked at his eight cards.

Elam looked at me.

I looked at Elam.

"B four," the man with the microphone said.

Hopp put a piece of corn on the square below the one he'd filled a few moments before.

"One more letter," Hopp said.

"I nineteen," the man with the microphone said.

"One more letter?" Elam said.

"And then what?" I said.

Hopp pointed to three of his eight cards, each of which was one letter short of spelling out the word BINGO in pieces of corn placed on numbers beneath the letters above.

"G sixty," the man with the microphone said.

"One more letter," Hopp said, pointing at the table of gifts right in front of us, "and that blender is mine."

I covered my eyes.

"The blender is yours," Elam said.

"One more letter," Hopp nodded.

The housewife next to me leaned over and said, bitterly, "He's already got a waffle iron, a toaster, a steam and dry iron and a set of coasters, and is he satisfied? No, he's got to have the blender, too."

Hopp pointed a finger at the housewife. "I told you to shut-up a long time ago, lady." He returned to his cards.

Elam was shaking his head.

I started playing an extra card that was in front of me.

Hopp said, "I haven't seen my wife in a year."

Elam said, "And you think a blender would make

her happy."

Hopp nodded.

"0 seventy," the man with the microphone said.

Elam said, "She wouldn't be satisfied with just a waffle iron."

"No," Hopp said.

"G forty-eight," the man with the microphone said.

Elam said, "She wouldn't be satisfied with just a toaster."

"No," Hopp said.

"B six," the man with the microphone said.

Elam said, "She wouldn't be satisfied with just a steam and dry iron."

"No," Hopp said.

"N forty-five," the man with the microphone said.

Elam said, "She wouldn't be satisfied with just a set of coasters."

"No," Hopp said.

"I sixteen," the man with the microphone said.

Elam said, "She's got to have the blender, too."

"Right," Hopp said.

"Bingo!" I said.

Tall thick shrubbery lined the edge of the park, with the graveled surface of the oil company storage depot area on one side and the back of the bandshell on the other. There was a small open area between the shrubbery and the bandshell, and that's where I met Sue Ann.

"I couldn't find your friend anywhere," she said.

I had sent her in search of Wheaty, while I went to round up Elam and Hopp, both of whom were now waiting by the stolen Mustang in front of the bank, waiting for me (and, hopefully, Wheat) to get us all out of here. I had watched from a distance as Elam and Hopp loaded Hopp's bingo loot (waffle iron, toaster, steam and dry iron, set of coasters and, yes, the blender, which I donated to the cause) into the back seat. I was rather glad about Hopp winning all that junk, as it might soften the blow a little when he found out later that the money from the bank robbery was *not* in the trunk of the Mustang, as Elam had told him, but still safely in the bank, sitting in laundry bags next to the trussed-up bank teller and Sue Ann's bank manager father.

Which leads us back into the bushes, or rather the open space between the bushes and the bandshell, where I was speaking to Sue Ann. Normally, it would've been pitch black in that open space, which was overhung by the shrubbery, but there was a full moon tonight and enough light was filtering down through the bushes for Sue Ann to see the incredulous look on my face when I heard her say she couldn't find Wheaty anywhere.

"He's around," I said. "I don't see how you could miss him."

"That's what I thought, so I asked some of my friends about him."

"You what?"

"I asked some of my friends if they'd seen him."

"Sue Ann, I asked you please not to do that. I said please just look for him yourself."

"I know, but what could it hurt?"

I was tempted to tell her, but managed to resist. Instead I said, "What did your friends say?"

"They saw him. He was with Becky all day."

"Who's Becky?"

"Becky Wynning. She's some distant relation of mine. I don't really know her too well. But you probably saw her this morning."

"Oh?"

"Sure. She's the Founder's Day Queen."

"Brown hair? Brown eyes? Tall? Big, uh . . . ?"

"The biggest," Sue Ann nodded. "Your friend and her were hanging all over each other, all day. But nobody's seen 'em for the last hour or so."

"Hmmm. Where does Becky Wynning live, Sue Ann? She and Wheat might've gone over to her house, to be alone or something. Is it close enough we could walk over and check?"

"Not really. She lives on a farm five or six miles outside of town."

"Damn. Does she have a car of her own?"

"I don't think so. I'm not really sure, though. Why, doesn't your friend have a car?"

"He does, but it's stuck in the middle of that street over there with a thousand other cars. Besides which, it's a Volkswagen and I doubt both Wheat and the king-size Queen could fit inside at the same time."

"Are you going to go looking for him, Fred?"

"I can't. No time for it."

"Why not?"

"Please, Sue Ann. I told you I couldn't explain everything. You just have to trust me. Believe me, I wouldn't risk something like this if there wasn't a good reason."

"Whatever the reason, it's exciting! I hope you won't mind me saying so, but I never met anybody with such . . . such . . . moxie!"

"Moxie?"

"It's an old-time word. Daddy uses it sometimes."

She would have to mention Daddy.

"Fred . . ."

"Yes?"

"Did you hear something?"

"When?"

"Now."

"No."

"I heard something."

"What?"

"Fred, you're shaking!"

"I'm running a quart low on moxie, Sue. Ann. What did you hear?"

"Sounded like somebody wrestling or something."

"Could you be more exact?"

"Well, I think I could."

"Be more exact."

"It sounded like a zipper."

"A zipper."

"You know what a zipper is, Fred."

"I know what a zipper is, and I also know you said you heard somebody wrestling, Sue Ann, and somebody wrestling doesn't sound like a zipper."

"The zipper was only part of it . . . wait . . . there, hear it?"

"No."

"A rustling sound. Wait. Listen. See if you hear anything."

I did, and I didn't.

"I think it was just your imagination, Sue Ann. Frankly, I don't see how you could hear a zipper with all that racket going on so close to us."

Over by the bank, the rock band was playing something loud and fast, while people danced in the streets and Elam and Hopp leaned against the stolen Mustang.

"I have excellent hearing, Fred. There! Don't you hear it?"

"More zippers?"

"More wrestling! Scuffling. Listen."

"Hey. Hey, yeah. It's coming from right over there."

"We better check it out, don't you think, Fred?"

"I'm not sure."

"I think we should."

She was right. If I was found here in the bushes with Sue Ann in a few minutes, when I was putting my idea into effect, I could really get caught with my pants down.

"Okay," I said. "Careful. It's coming from under

the bandstand, isn't it? Is that possible?"

"Yes. It's hollow underneath. Shhh. They'll hear us."

Then I saw the feet.

Four of them, to be exact.

The four feet were naked. That is, had no shoes or socks on.

And I was suddenly embarrassed.

What else would the hollow area beneath a park bandshell be used for on a summer evening but making out? The sounds of kissing and cuddling and assorted affection prompted me to try and tug Sue Ann's sleeve so we could retreat before my embarrassment was passed along to the happy couple under the bandshell, who as yet hadn't noticed us creeping up on them.

Then I took a closer look at the four feet and recognized them. Two of them, anyway. The other two feet I could pretty well figure out. All four of the feet were large, though two of them were more feminine than the others. Large feet belonging to large people.

Wheaty and the Founder's Day Queen.

"Wheat!" I whispered. "It's me! Kitch!"

"Kitch!" Wheat said, sitting up, bumping his head on the roof (or rather, floor) of the bandshell.

"Wheat, get out of there. It's important."

"Well, gee, so is this, Kitch."

The toes belonging to the Founder's Day Queen had long since curled, and I now heard some terrified whispering from the Queen who had been quite understandably scared out of her socks (figuratively speaking) by the interruption.

First Wheat, then the Queen, peeked out. Neither Wheat or the Queen was undressed, just disheveled, unbuttoned, and, well, let's just say there was nothing wrong with Sue Ann's hearing. The Queen just sat there in her fetchingly disarrayed white dress (which was looking less and less virginal all the time) and tried to straighten her rhinestone tiara and blushed. Sue Ann apologized for our rude interruption, and said not to be embarrassed, because "Fred and I have been making out all afternoon ourselves."

Everybody blushed then (except Sue Ann, of course) and Wheat asked me what was going on.

I said, "We're going to help our friends get out of town."

Surprisingly, Wheat understood at once. "Good," he said. "How?"

"I'll explain later. For right now, just do what I tell you, and trust me."

"Sure, Kitch. I suppose I better be getting my shoes back on, huh?"

"Not exactly," I said, and I took off my clothes and handed them to Sue Ann.

"My mom'll kill me," Wheat said.

We were both crouched in the bushes at the edge of the park, a few feet away from the main street and the crowd of people who were still enthusiastically celebrating Founder's Day. Right now there was a lull while the rock band left the stage (that is, the platform truck) and the country western band took over; the two bands had been alternating since late this afternoon. The country western band was getting its guitars slung around its necks and what not, and the pudgy, bald Mayor of Wynning was standing at the microphone announcing the winners of various events of the day, including the watermelon-eating contest, in which Sue Ann's police chief Uncle Phil had come in second. I could see two of the reporters were still with us, the one from the *Port City Journal* and the one from the *Des Moines Register*, too. Both of them had their flash cameras out and were taking pictures of things, the Mayor at the moment; both of them seemed thoroughly sloshed on the nickel beer the local bar was still dispensing. There were still a lot of people here, in fact I'd guess just about everybody had stayed the duration: when the rock band was playing, the adults would stand along the sidelines (and sit, as many of them had brought lounge chairs along) and watch the kids dance; and when the country western band was playing, the kids would disappear off into the park and find a tree (or a bandshell) to neck under. A lot of the people were munching on tacos or snow cones or cotton candy, or drinking pop or the nickel beer. Everybody seemed to be enjoying themselves. What I'm saying is, Founder's Day gave no signs of letting up. It could go on this way till midnight. Tomorrow.

Wheat and I crouched in the bushes and took all this in. Did I mention we were naked?

We were naked.

Standing over in the crowd, leaning against the stolen Mustang, slurping good-naturedly at nickel beer, doing their best to look inconspicuous and not doing a bad job of it, were Elam and Hopp. Elam was watching the bushes, as I'd told him to. I stuck my head out a ways. A little ways. Elam nodded that he'd seen me and I stuck my head back in.

"My mom'll kill me, Kitch," Wheat said again.

"She didn't kill you last time."

"Almost."

"We got no choice, Wheat. You think I like this idea?"

"You think I want to go back to jail, Kitch?"

"You didn't seem to mind the first time."

"At least explain why we're doing this."

The two Highway Patrolmen were leaning against their car, looking bored. One of them was eating a grape snow cone. The other was slouched, arms folded, half-asleep.

"No time to explain, Wheat," I said. "Let's go."

And two naked birds, with nothing in hand, emerged from the bush.

Running.

I took the lead.

This time I wasn't covering myself. It wasn't that I'd gotten over my initial shyness: there were people to push through. We literally had to shove our way through the crowd to be able to run in front of the platform truck where the Mayor was announcing the winners of the bake-off.

It wasn't as bad as coming through those doors and unexpectedly bumping into a wedding party assembled for a picture taking. No, this time Wheat and I were ready for the throng, and neither one of us fell down. We did get our pictures taken again, though, as both drunken reporters managed to snap their flash cameras and catch us as we streaked by.

I caught a glimpse of a Highway Patrolman dropping a snow cone to the pavement as we passed, cutting within three feet of the patrol car. I heard squeals of laughter and horror and even some scattered applause as we cut around the platform truck and skirted the saw-horse blocking off the main street from where it turned into the highway out of town, which is where we headed.

I heard Wheat coming up from behind me, and then he was edging up on me, and we were like a couple of relay runners who forgot to bring along a baton to pass. There was no sound, except for our feet on the blacktop road, and our breathing. It wasn't dark out at all, the moon was bathing us and the road in a milky glow. We were running like graceful animals, side by side, in perfect precision. We were running fast, hard, but easily, too, like conditioned athletes.

We were beautiful.

It was so different this time. I felt no sense of panic, or even of danger. I felt free. Naked and running and free, my feet padding along the road, cornfields gliding by on either side of me, the moon coasting along above.

I looked over at Wheat, not breaking stride.

He was grinning.

I grinned back at him, and we stepped up the pace a little. By that time we'd gone a good half mile.

By that time the siren had started up, and the Highway Patrol car was in pursuit.

A quarter mile later they caught us.

The Highway Patrolman who hours earlier had reminded me of Shaker Saltz grabbed me by the arm. The other patrolman grabbed Wheat's arm, and both of them solemnly shoved us in back and drove us wordlessly back into Wynning.

We were greeted with cheers and applause. There were a few sour faces in the crowd, but not many. The Mayor looked confused, but I saw Uncle Phil, who was grinning ear to ear, and then saw him lean over and begin whispering in the Mayor's ear, and the Mayor began to nod. Most of the townspeople were too high on nickel beer and tacos and snow cones and cotton candy and pop to be mad at us. Sue Ann came over to where the patrol car had pulled up and blew me a kiss through the window. She had my clothes under her arm.

It pleased me to come back to such a warm reception. But it pleased me even more to come back and see that empty space along the curb in front of the bank.

Nobody pressed any charges. Sue Ann's uncle convinced the Mayor that Wheat and me streaking was a positive thing for Wynning, that it would mean just that much more publicity for the Centennial Celebration.

Which was exactly right. The *Des Moines Register* guy's picture came out over-exposed, but the *Port City Journal* photographer got a good clear shot of us, which he sold to *People* magazine, who did an article on us, which stated that we had streaked at Wynning to protest our going to jail for the other time we streaked. I told them that, and it was a lie. I admit it.

By now I'm sure you understand why we streaked. First off it gave Wheat and me a reason for being in Wynning. Sue Ann's uncle, seeing me there, assumed I had come to streak, and I couldn't let him down, without making him suspicious. And, of course, streaking we drew away the highway patrol and enabled Elam and Hopp to sneak out of Wynning by the back door.

And in case you're wondering how I convinced Elam to go along with leaving the money behind, I simply pointed out that a thorough investigation of the bank robbery (and with the money taken, the investigation would be far more thorough than if not) would have had to include an investigation of Wheat and me and why we were in Wynning, and from Wheat and me to our DeKalb County Jail bunkmates Elam and Hopp would be no great jump.

But we never were linked to the robbery. If you can even call it a robbery: after all, no money was taken. And I wouldn't have written this book if my lawyer hadn't advised me that no legal action was likely to be taken against me.

Sue Ann's father will be finding out the truth for the first time when he reads this. I expect his reaction to be negative. He's a nice man, but he's bound to be unhappy about being bound for fifteen some hours in that bank.

Sue Ann I did tell that truth to, and right away. She found it all very exciting, and didn't feel I'd taken advantage of her in the least. Otherwise we probably wouldn't be married and living together in Iowa City right now. I am going to grad school, in business, and her father is helping me through, though he may cut me off when he reads this book.

I also told the truth to my father, who at first was furious with me, for all kinds of reasons; but then I reminded him he was a minister and said, "Come on, Dad . . . all I did was turn the other cheek," and he started laughing and forgave me. My mother gave in (and stopped crying) when she saw me on *The Mike Douglas Show*. If Mike Douglas wasn't ashamed of me, well, then, she wasn't ashamed of me, either.

Of course Wheaty has done much better on the talk show circuit than I have. We did several of them together (we did *The Tomorrow Show* with the guy who streaked the Academy Awards) and then they started asking Wheaty alone. Johnny Carson has had Wheaty on six times, one of which was when Johnny himself was there. Wheat's living in Hollywood, with the Founder's Day Queen.

Wheaty and I are a corporation, as you may have read. We each get half of each other's project. I get half of his comedy album, and he gets half of this book. Wheat and I are still the best of friends, contrary to what you may have read in the *National Enquirer*.

Now comes the hard part. Ending the story. My agent wanted me to call in a ghost writer to help on this book, primarily because he wanted to have the manuscript in about two weeks, before the streaking fad became ancient history, but I insisted on doing it all myself, and not trying to just rush through and cash in on a fad.

But I really do wish I could have a professional writer's help right now, because the story is over, and I don't know what to do to get off stage.

Sue Ann is standing behind me, as I sit here typing this, and she's impatient for me to finish.

She doesn't have any clothes on.

Which is the moral of this story, I guess: taking your clothes off can be very rewarding, if you play your cards right.

Public Servant

I felt great, my heart was pounding, but I should have slugged her harder. Or killed her, one of the two. I was hardly out the window and onto the lawn when she woke up and started in screaming her head off.

"Shut up, you bitch . . ." My voice hissed through my teeth like air from a punctured tire. "I'll hit you again, Goddamnit, shut the fuck up."

But it was too late.

Too late to climb back in and shut her up and too late to get away. I moved past the bushes along the side of the house and went back to my car in the alley. I could hear voices only a block or so away, so I had to work fast. I pulled the tactic I'd thought about a few times but never used. I reached in the back seat and grabbed my holstered gun, blue shirt with badge, and cap. Put them on faster than hell. Then I reached around into the front seat and flipped on the radio and grabbed off the mike and spoke into it.

"Ralph, hello Ralph, this is Harry."

His voice came back tinny over the cheap squawk-box speakers. "What's the trouble, officer?"

The mayor must have been in the station or Ralph wouldn't have called me "officer." Ralph was the chief but we didn't have many formalities, not in a town of a few thousand.

"Look, Ralph, I think the raper's hit again. There's a woman screaming and I'm heading over to look into it. Okay, Ralph?"

He forgot the newfound formality fast. "Jesus H. Christ, another rape! Damn it, damn. Any sign of the bastard?"

"Ralph, I'll shoot the damn bull with you some other time, okay? I'm going over and see what the hell's going on, you don't mind."

"I better send somebody over to help you."

"Good idea."

"Frank's hanging around the building some-where. He's off duty, but he's the only one here so I'll send him."

"We're going to get this guy, Ralph."

"Damn right we will, Harry."

I clicked the mike off and put it back on the radio and headed for the house. Things'd been happening fast. Almost forgot to zip my fly.

She was still screaming, so I didn't go in. Besides, there was a crowd of people in bathrobes and dressing gowns and such milling around, and I had to keep them cleared away as best I could till Frank got there to lend a hand.

When Frank finally did show, I told him to go in and do the questioning. An ambulance, Frank said, was on the way. I stood outside and worked at moving the funseekers away.

After a while the ambulance pulled up and I went inside and helped Frank and some guy from the hospital ease the bitch onto a stretcher and out the door and into the back of the ambulance. She looked right at me once and didn't bat an eye. The ambulance tore away and Frank stood there looking after it, shaking his head.

"Damn that bastard anyway, Harry, that damn bastard's going to get his, I swear."

"Same guy, suppose?"

"Sure as hell is. Same as always. Woman at home alone, her husband on the night shift or off on a National Guard stint or something of the like. The son of a bitch jimmies open a window and attacks her in her sleep, then knocks hell out of her."

"Have a cigarette, Frank."

Frank was in civvies, a T-shirt and white jeans as a matter of fact, and he stood there looking toward where the ambulance'd been, rubbing his hand over the place on his sandy crewcut where it was thinning. He said "Thanks" when I handed him the cigarette and lit it off his own lighter.

"You ain't letting this thing get you, are you, Frank?"

"Guess maybe I am. Jesus, let me tell you, it's enough to scare hell out of a married man. Christ, I mean you, you aren't married, you can't understand just how bad it is. But me, hell. A young wife. A kid in a crib. Me gone nights a lot. Scares the crap right out of me, a nut like this loose."

"Sure, Frank," I said. "I can see what you mean. I mean, I ain't married or anything, but I can see what you mean."

Frank rubbed his eyes with the heels of his hands. "Hell, Harry, how do you figure him? A psycho, sure, but how do you figure him?"

I smiled. "How *do* you figure a psycho?"

"I don't know. I honest to God don't know. But he gets his jollies making people hurt, I can see that plain enough. He always slugs hell out of the women, after he's had 'em. Didn't beat this as bad as the others, though, did you notice? Must be getting careless or something. Getting used to getting away with it. I mean, shit, we make it easy enough for him with our Mickey Mouse force."

"We're doing our best, Frank, ain't we?"

"Yeah. Our best. Dedicated public servants. Yeah."

He arched the hardly smoked cigarette out into the street.

"He'll probably be more careful next time, you know," I said.

"No next time about it," he said, "not if I can help it."

"Know what you mean, Frank, I mean wouldn't you just like to get this bastard down and kick the hell out of him?"

Seemed like Frank's eyes were almost glowing. "That would be sweet. That sure as Christ would be sweet."

I patted his shoulder. "Well, we'll get him, Frank, don't you worry. I mean, after all, you figure him a nut, how long can a nut last?"

"Oh, but a damn smart nut, remember. There's never a fingerprint or clue of any kind around."

I checked my watch. "I wonder what's keeping Ollie with that damn Boy Scout crime lab of his? He ought to be here by now."

Frank shrugged. "Probably so used to this he's finishing the *Late Show* or something before he comes over. Besides, what's the use? That nut's a thinker, he never leaves anything to trace him. Anyway, nothing a small-scale set-up like we got could ever pick up on."

I lit myself a smoke. "But like you said, he's getting more careless. Had so much fun raping this one he didn't slug her as hard as he should've. Maybe this time he slipped up."

"Maybe you're right, Harry. Maybe old Ollie'll find something this time around."

"Here, Frank, have another smoke." I shook one out of the pack and fired him up off my lighter. "Stay out here and relax, I'll go back in, and make sure none of the neighbors messed anything up before we got here."

Frank nodded. I went back in and looked around.

Wiped off the windowsill with my handkerchief, a few other things, too. Had to make sure I wasn't getting too damn careless.

When I was on night duty I'd go to bed around nine o'clock in the morning and sleep till six or seven. Then I'd go over to the Seaside Motel to see Molly, and sometimes sponge a meal off her. Molly was sort of my girl. She thought she was, at least. She ran the Seaside, which is right by the lake. Her old man, who built the place (both him and the old lady kicked off in an auto wreck five, six years back), would've called it the Lakeside instead of the Seaside, only somebody else on the other side of town thought of it first. And the other motel wasn't even on the damn lake, ain't *that* the shits.

The "No Vacancy" sign wasn't on because the Seaside's whole neon system'd blown a few months before. But a wooden sign hung in the window of the office saying no dice to any travelers. Not that many stopped, only the regular round of salesmen who filled the Seaside's seven dumpy little cabins during the week and the teenagers and college kids who used 'em on weekends.

The door was locked but I had a key. I went on in to Molly's living quarters beyond the office. She wasn't around. Probably down the hill by the lake.

The night air was chilly, though it was summer, high summer. Of course it's always cool on the lake, nights. I don't like the lake much. It's pretty, like a picture in a travel book, with the neon reflected on the rippling water and all that sort of shit. I'm not much for pretty things, except for pretty things like Molly. Or most any woman.

Down the gravel hill path and onto the beach I went, keeping my hand over the holstered rod at all times. Never could tell when somebody would catch up with me and then all my fun and games'd be over. So I kept my hand over the rod constant, so I could take the pleasure of blowing out some guy's guts before they took me. Sure they said I was a nut, a psycho (don't you believe it!) but I was having a hell of a good time being one.

Molly was standing on the beach in a blouse and loose skirt that was blowing up over her thighs in the gentle lake breeze. She was looking out onto the picture-book lake, watching the easy movement of the waves.

She'd heard me coming, knew I was there without looking around.

"Hi Harry. Nice night."

"Hi."

"How about some supper? I could go back up and fix us some."

I didn't answer her right away, so she turned and looked at me.

She was pretty, pretty near, her nice hazel-blue eyes the best part about her. Her hair was all right, too, for being all bleached out.

"Well, Harry, what do you say? Is it going to be supper? It's a really nice night, maybe you just want to go for a row or something?"

I grabbed her at the waist, pulled her in close to me.

"A row, Harry? How's that sound? The boat's tied down at the dock. Come on, Harry, what do you want to do?"

I squeezed. Tight. "Trouble with you, Molly, is that you don't know when to shut up. You shouldn't talk so damn much."

"Harry . . ." She laughed. I was squeezing her so hard it must have hurt like hell, but she only laughed. "Jesus, you're mean, Harry, you're one mean son of a bitch."

I squeezed even harder. "And that's what you like about me, ain't it, baby?"

She threw back her head and laughed some more. "You're goddamn right, Harry, you're goddamn right."

I latched onto her blouse and ripped it half off in one yank.

"Hey, you bastard! Take it easy on the clothes."

"What's wrong, honey? Thought you liked your Harry to be mean."

She stood there and the cold got at her, turning her blue and goose-pimply. She clutched her arms over her breasts and her teeth chattered as she said, "Be . . . be-being mean's one thing, Har . . . Harry . . . But wasting my damn m . . . money like that's an . . . another."

I wasn't worried, even if I'd cost her some in torn clothes and the like. What the hell. I reached for her skirt to rip that off her, too, but she jumped out of reach.

"Damn you, Harry! Damn you!" But she wasn't as mad as she was acting. "I'll unhook it, damn it, don't rip it off!"

She got out of the skirt before I could get my hands on it. She walked up to me and I slugged her right in the teeth and she went down like soft rope. I gripped her shoulders and pulled her up and bit into her mouth.

"Oh . . . Oh, Jesus, Harry, I love you . . ."

I laughed and bit into her bloody lips again. I liked the taste.

After I left Molly's I stopped at the diner along Fourth Street for a bite to eat. Usually I ate at Molly's, but she had this thing about if I came to supper, fine, I can have supper and what else I wanted after, but if I took what else first, I could go out and buy my own damn chow after.

The counterman's name was Lou and he said, "Evening, Harry, what's it to be?"

"Gimme number two on the breakfasts, Lou."

I sat down on a stool at the counter and brushed the crumbs away from in front of me. A guy sat next to me sipping at his coffee. He turned and smiled and started in to talking like people do to cops sometimes, like they're trying to get in good with them or something. He sounded like a salesman; they're always getting friendly with cops. That's how a lot of them find a woman for the night in towns. But you'd think a guy could tell just looking at me I'm no goddamn pimp. Anyway, he starts in to talking:

"You always have breakfast here, officer, at eight

o'clock in the evening like this?"

"Sure I do, mister, if I don't eat at my girl's place."

"Why breakfast? Any special reason, or you just like it?"

"I'm on night duty this week, pal, just got up. So I'm having breakfast."

"Oh." Back to his coffee for a minute, then: "Hear you've been having some trouble around here lately."

"Yeah," I said, trying not to get pissed at the guy; I hate pests, but I had to grin and bear it with guys like this so's folks wouldn't find out about the "beast" in me. "Yeah, trouble."

"I don't envy you guys on night duty when there's a lunatic running loose. You work in pairs, surely?"

"Nope. Can't afford to. Ain't enough men to go around."

"One man to a car? You have a small force, huh?"

"Yeah, the wages for a cop ain't worth crap."

"Pay is low, huh? That's the trouble everywhere. It's a wonder they find decent guys like you to take the job, fella."

"Thanks, pal."

"When a town pays low wages to cops, lots of times it attracts scum. You know, some nut who wants to wear a uniform and a badge. And carry a gun and a club."

I turned around on my stool and looked the guy over. A short guy in a brown suit, with small blue eyes in an oval face and receding gray-brown hair. Little punk.

I said, "I don't mean to be nasty, mister, but don't put cops down, okay? They get paid nothing while they work their tails off for the public. Jesus, the b.s. people hand out to cops! How would you like to be a cop where there's a psycho loose? You got some nerve, buddy, some nerve, you and all the others who don't appreciate what cops do for you. Police brutality, police brutality, that's all we get from Mister Public. Why, it wouldn't be safe to walk the streets at night without us suckers in blue to do the dirty work for John Q. Citizen."

The guy was sort of shaking now, spilled a little of his coffee. "Look . . . look . . . I didn't mean anything . . . I just think you guys should get paid better, that's all. That's all."

I smiled at him, both rows of whites. "Want sugar'n cream in your coffee, pal?"

He nodded nervously. I passed them to him and he poured a touch of each into his cup, then started in stirring, still nervous-like.

"I always take sugar'n cream in mine," I said. "Can't stand coffee black. Too damn bitter."

My breakfast came and I started in on it, three pancakes, two sausages, some scrambled eggs, milk, and coffee. The guy next to me went through a hamburger and fries. Or tried to anyway. He was so damn nervous he could hardly swallow a bite. I convinced him to stay on with me for another cup of coffee. After a bit we started in walking out of the diner together, having gotten more palsy with each other.

Out in the cold night air he put a hand on my shoulder and said, "You seem like a decent guy to me, officer. I didn't mean for you to take offense back there or anything. I just meant for you to see how I felt about cops getting paid bad. I mean, they should pay you guys more and keep out the riffraff, is what I mean. Those guys that just want to be a cop so they can hurt people and get away with it, you know, wear a blue suit and badge and carry a gun. No offense, right?"

I said sure. Did he want a lift?

"Well . . . my hotel's just a couple blocks, officer."

"Come on, I'll take ya there."

"Well . . . oh hell, okay."

He climbed into the front seat of the car. He fiddled around with the call box under the middle part of the dashboard like a kid in a toy shop. I began to think he'd had a little to drink or something, the way he fooled with things and the way his mouth was slack. But I couldn't tell for sure. Anyway, I got in and started the car.

"I'm staying at the Carleton, officer."

"My name's Harry. Wish you'd call me Harry."

"Sure, Harry. Mine's Joe, Joe Comstock. Salesman. Never been here before."

"We got a nice little town here. Friendly."

"Say, uh, Harry, I'm at the Carleton."

"Yeah, Joe, I know that."

"Well, uh, that's the other way . . . down the street that way . . ."

"I thought maybe we'd go riding for a while, Joe. I sure could use a little spot of company. Nothing wrong with a little ride is there, Joe?"

"Oh . . . no. Okay. Sure. Hell, I got nothing else to do."

He lit a cigarette and we drove in silence for a while. Then he came up with the best yet:

"You know, Harry, I been thinking. About this low pay for cops bit? Why, hell, Harry, what with the low pay luring the kooks and sadist-types, these eight rapes you've had here over the past few months? Guy in a bar told me about them this afternoon, you know. Those eight rapes?"

I kept my eyes on the road. "Yeah?"

"What with the low salaries and all, the rapist, don't you think he . . . well, hell, he could even be a cop."

I didn't say anything.

"I don't mean anything against cops, mind you, Harry, you know that, I explained that. . . . But don't you think that could be possible?"

I braked the car.

"What are you stopping for?"

"Get out of the car, Joe."

He opened the door and climbed out; I got out and walked around the car and motioned him over toward the bushes. He started looking around but he didn't see nothing but trees and bushes and empty highway and night. I went over and clutched him by the arm.

"Now, Joe," I said, nice and friendly like, walking him along, "let me tell you the real reason I brung you out here. You look like a fella I saw on a wanted circular at the station the other day. Now since you seem like a right guy, I brung you out here where you ain't likely to be embarrassed. So now talk to me like a brother and tell me who you really are."

His mouth dropped open. "Hell, Harry, I'm just a salesman."

"The truth . . ."

"Harry . . . hell, Harry . . ."

"Put your hands in the air."

He shrugged and put them up. I swung a hard right to his groin. He rolled up into a little ball and made crying sounds. Then I got him by the scruff of the neck and dragged him behind the clump of bushes, where we wouldn't be seen if a car happened by on the highway. He kept on crying as I'd hit him pretty hard and I proceeded in to kicking him a few times while I fished out my big revolver. I spent a good five minutes whipping him with the gun butt. He made some sounds but didn't say anything, except "Jesus," once, just before he died.

The rest of the night was quiet.

That was my last shift of night duty before the weekend, which I got free. I'd be back to days starting Monday, always got a free weekend after working seven nights straight.

I stopped in at the station to see the chief. It's not much as stations go, really, just one room in the city hall basement. It's a white-walled room with lots of dirt rubbed in; only part that doesn't show the dirty

white walls is the part covered by the big bulletin
board with the wanted posters and the like plastered
to it. The chief sits in one corner behind a desk piled
high with papers and a file cabinet on each end like
two big bookends holding him in. That's about it for
our station, except for our traffic officer who's got a
real small office all to himself and the tons of unpaid
tickets. Also there are a few cells adjoining the one
main room. Otherwise, there's only Jim Oliver, a guy
who is a technician of some kind out at the hospital
and tries to help with our "scientific methods" since
our force ain't exactly crime lab size. Mostly Ollie
has been a joke with us.

Anyway, I stopped in to see the chief.

"Hiya, Ralph," I said, both rows of white on parade.

"Hi, Harry." Ralph didn't look up from the paper
he was reading. He was in his TV cop mood today, I
could tell right off. Chewing on a cigar and not smiling. Rubbing a hand over his bald spot and tweaking
his bulbous nose once in a while. Maybe he pictured
himself like a TV cop, since he had an actual case on
his hands for the first time. The rapes, I mean.

"Got anything on the raper yet?" I asked him.

"Nope. Not a damn thing. Ollie tried looking
around that place the other night but, hell, he doesn't
do any good. I wish some of the state cops'd help out."

"Ain't their affair. 'Sides, Ralph, they wouldn't do
much better than old Ollie."

"Sure they would. The bastard'd get his if there was
some kind of responsible-type investigation made.

But there's not much chance of that in this town."

I shook my head in concern. "It's an outright shame a nut like that runs loose. A damn shame. Too bad the feds ain't in on it."

Ralph smiled around the cigar. "Damn right. They'd crack this thing in a hurry, wouldn't they? But how the hell would the FBI get in on a local deal like this? Rape's no federal offense."

I shrugged, said, "No chance of the feds coming in, I guess. But this lad'd get caught real soon if somebody who knew what they was doing was after him, 'stead of us."

Ralph shook his head. "Sometimes I wish I would have stayed over at the cigar store, but I thought this job'd prove easier."

With a grin, I lit up a cigarette and said, "It would have if this sex nut hadn't't've turned up."

"He's not so nuts, Harry."

"Oh, no, he's not nuts, he just rapes and kills."

"Kills?"

"Well, damn near kills. You know what I mean."

"Yeah. Well, I don't think he's a nut all the way, you know. After all, he picked a town where he'll like as not get away with all of it."

"Maybe, Ralph. How about pouring me some of that coffee?"

There was a pitcher of hot coffee on his desk, from which he kindly poured me a cup.

"You know, Ralph," I said, taking the cup from him, "there's a joke been going around town lately."

"That a fact?"

"Uh-huh. It's about this girl who was married three times and was still a virgin. Know how she managed that? First she married a midget, see, and he was too small. Next she married a preacher, and he was too religious. Then she married a small-town cop, and he couldn't find it."

Ralph laughed and said, "There's more truth than poetry in that one, Harry."

"Got sugar?" I asked. "And cream? I always take sugar'n cream. Coffee's way too bitter without 'em." *It was a pity* what happened with Molly.

It was a couple weeks later, I was back on the night shift and the night before I'd pulled off number nine, a plump blonde bitch whose hubby was off at reserve camp. It had been awful quiet on the day shift, no one had found the salesman's body. They were all too busy worrying about rape number eight. Now that rape number nine'd come along, I figured that would give everybody something else to worry about for a while.

But I was wrong.

Because that night when we were sitting together down on the beach, Molly dropped a bombshell and told me she figured me for the raper.

"You're wrong, Molly, dead wrong. I didn't ever lay a hand on any woman but you."

"You're lying to me, Harry, I know you are." Her eyes looked green in the light of the quarter moon. I smoothed a hand over her arm as gentle as I could, but she jerked away and looked out toward the water. The lake was smooth, with only a few easy waves.

"Nice night, ain't it?" I said. "Be a nice night for a row."

"I don't . . . I don't feel like a row tonight, Harry. I don't . . . don't know anymore."

I grabbed a handful of her hair and pulled her head back—real gentle-like, of course—and said, "Molly, honey, would I ever think of touching another woman? You think I'd need to force a woman to get love off her?"

She pulled away again and started drawing in the sand with her finger.

"You ain't listening to me, Molly."

She kept on drawing in the sand. She seemed like maybe she was crying, but her voice was steady. "You're a funny man, Harry. You like your love to hurt. You're all take and not a damn bit of give."

I gripped her arm, hard, and she yelped a little. "You're dead wrong, Molly," I said again. "Let me prove it to you. Go out for a row with me. Come on. I love you, Molly, you'll see. Come on out for a row."

She stood up, circling her bare feet in the sand. Her face looked almost beautiful streaked with tears the way it was. "You're all I've got, Harry . . . I guess, if I'm right in what I say about you, then I don't want to live anymore. And if I'm wrong about you, well, then things'd be okay again. But even then, even if you didn't rape those women, it'll be bad, though, won't it? You and me just aren't right, Harry, so I guess things couldn't ever be fine, or good. Cause just like you like to hurt me, I like getting hurt by you, Harry . . . and that's not right. But if you . . . if you haven't been the one doing all those bad things around town, then a little boat ride wouldn't hurt, would it?"

"Why, course not."

"But if you were the one raping and all, then I probably wouldn't be coming back from that little boat ride, would I?"

"That's right, Molly. If I was."

"But if not . . ."

"Then it wouldn't hurt nothing at all, Molly, nothing at all. Come on, it's a nice night. Come on."

She turned and headed for the dock down the beach where the rowboat was tied. Her hair looked nice in the moonlight. She had nice legs when she walked, too.

We untied the boat, then I kicked off my shoes and together we waded into the water and pushed the boat out a ways. We climbed in and I started rowing. She didn't look at me, just stared out at the reflection of the quarter moon on the glassy surface of the lake.

About halfway out I threw her over, held her head down till she drowned. She didn't fight it at all. The place where she went under rippled out for a while, like a target, then got smooth again.

Later on I stopped at the diner on Fourth Street. I ordered a breakfast from the counterman, Lou, and started reading the evening paper.

Lou brought me my coffee and said, "Those guys

ever find you, Harry?"

"What guys?"

A voice from behind me said, "Hiya, Harry."

"Well, Frank, how the hell're you? Going on duty soon?"

"Yeah, in a few minutes. You just finishing up your shift, huh?"

"That's right. How've ya been?" I hadn't seen much of Frank lately, since that night a while back when I had to stick around and play cop after that one deal. Should have hit that bitch harder.

"Been rough, Harry, what with my regular tours of duty and trying to look into this rapist thing in my spare time."

"Any luck?"

"Not a bit."

Frank was a small guy, but even a heel like me couldn't help but take a shine to the son of a bitch. He was everything a cop ought to be, honest and family-loving and all like that. Only his clean living was taking wear, putting deep lines in his face, around his clear blue eyes, and it seemed like his sandy crewcut was starting back farther on his head every time I saw him.

"Say, Harry," Frank said, "did you hear about the guy on the highway?"

I put down the paper. "What guy?"

"State cops found a dead guy out here along the highway a couple weeks ago, hushed it all up, not even the chief knew about it."

"Oh, really? Ain't that something." Lou was there with my breakfast, but all of a sudden I wasn't hungry

"That's what I was trying to tell you about, Harry," Lou said, putting the food down in front of me.

"What?"

"Those two FBI men was in asking about that little guy you was talking to in here a couple weeks ago. That little guy, remember? He was the one got killed, I guess."

"FBI?" I said.

"Yeah," Frank chimed in, "seems this guy was important or something. Joker was a government courier of some kind."

"Govern . . . government courier?" I took a sip of my coffee as casually as I could.

"These FBI guys are putting on a full-scale investigation," Frank said. "I talked to them this afternoon, before they started going 'round town to ask questions. Too bad we can't get them to work on this rapist deal while they're at it."

"Yeah, too bad."

"What's this about you seeing that guy the night he was killed? And right here in the diner?"

"Oh, uh, I was just . . ."

Lou said, "Haven't you talked to those guys yet, Harry? I sent 'em out to your girl's place, figured you'd be out there at the Seaside with Molly. You must've just missed 'em."

I took another swallow of the coffee and tried to think.

"What's wrong, Harry?" Frank said.

"Hell," Lou laughed, slapping the counter, "he's drinking his coffee black. What's with you, Harry? You know you can't stomach it without cream and sugar."

THE LOVE RACK

I guess I'm resigned to the fact that I'm going to die. Or as resigned to dying as a man can get, anyway. They've told me, you see, that they're going to kill me. And I have no reason to doubt them. It's as simple as that.

Haven't eaten in quite a while but I'm not overly hungry. Wonder if it matters if you die on an empty stomach? At least there won't be anything left in me to embarrass anybody. I hear a man's bowels clean themselves out once he's dead, and I'd hate like hell to be an embarrassing corpse.

I have had a woman, though, and not long ago. A very beautiful woman, too, with soft gold hair and warm brown eyes. Yes, yes, I've known her that way, I've had that much. Seems as if we made love all night long. Wonderful. I've got no complaints about that part of it. Haven't known her long but I could love her if I had a while, I think. Hell, maybe I love her right now.

Her face is her face, but it's also someone else's. From a long time ago. It's all very confusing.

She lies still, not far from me, as though she were dead.

Perhaps she is.

After a while it gets kind of hard to remember....

In the evening I went out with a young woman who wouldn't. I dropped her off at her place and went back out into the city and got lost for a while and drank. Don't own a car, so I walked the streets rather than take a cab. I don't live far from the downtown anyway. It had been raining and the streets were shiny black like patent leather. Once I almost got hit when I decided to look at my reflection in the funny black mirror which turned out to be the middle of the funny black street. I called the driver who nearly clipped me a motherfucker - I sober up quickly - and tottered off in the vague direction of my apartment.

I got back around two or three in the morning. Not drunk, mind you, but not ready to take on a high wire act either.

I went into the bedroom, stripped down to my shorts, flopped down on the bed. Thought sleep would come easy, but no go. My head ached, and badly. Migraines hit me from time to time, and this was a time.

Got to sleep in an hour or so.

I dreamed. I dreamed I was spread out on a long wooden frame, my legs and arms tied to the ends of it. Then a girl, young and pretty, with the face of someone I loved once, began to twist a wheel which caused the frame to extend and started pulling my limbs apart from my body. I just lay there on the rack and screamed while she kept working the wheel, her face chiseled stone.

I awoke in a cold sweat, naturally, and shook off the damn thing as quickly as I could, before rolling over and back to sleep again. I had had to get used to the dream, because I'd had it as an unwanted bed partner for years.

When I got back to sleep the dream took over again and just as my right arm was being slowly stretched free of my shoulder, someone started playing kettle drums outside.

I sat up in bed.

Knocking. Someone at the door.

I said, "Damn," and got up and threw on my trousers and kept on saying "Damn" till I reached the door.

When I opened it I found a man about my size, though not quite as heavy as I am, waiting for me patiently. He wore a rather handsome tweed overcoat and an air of having made it big in something or other. The only real catch was the undernourished look he had, complete with chalk-cheeked face with vein-lined bones jutting out from it at sharp angles. Also he seemed vaguely familiar, like something from an old newsreel, and he was smiling like a long-lost brother.

He said, "Hello, Smitty."

"Okay. Hello. Who the hell're you?"

"It's been a while. Don't you remember?"

"No."

"Aren't you going to ask me in, take my coat?"

"No."

"Now, come on, Smitt..."

"Who the hell're you?"

"It's Vin, Smitt, Vin, don't you know me?"

"Vin. Thompson? Vin Thompson?"

"Korea wasn't that long ago, was it?"

"It's been long enough."

"Am I disturbing you?"

"Oh no, everybody drops in at three in the morning."

"I didn't wake up the wife or kids, did I?"

"I'm not married and don't have any kids that I know of."

"You didn't marry that girl back home? That Karen?"

"No. I got a letter from her while I was still over there. Married somebody else, the bitch."

"Sorry, Smitt."

"Don't be."

"Well, Smitty?"

"Well what?"

"Aren't you going to ask me in?"

"No."

"Smitty, we fought together."

"The hell we did. I was a lieutenant and you were a lieutenant colonel. I barely knew you. Besides, ask me if I give a damn about all that army shit."

"Do you, Smitt? Do you give a damn?"

That didn't deserve an answer. I started to close the door on this unwanted ghost when he reached into one of the large pockets on the handsome tweed coat. When his hand came back it had an automatic in it.

"Okay," I said, suddenly giving a damn, "come on in."

"Good to see you, Smitt. Close the door, will you?"

"Drop dead."

He shrugged and kicked it shut.

I rubbed by eyes, belched, and collapsed on the davenport.

"You tired or something, Smitt?"

"What makes you think that?"

A deck of cigarettes appeared in Vin's hand from out the other kangaroo's pouch on the tweed coat. He gave himself a cigarette and tossed another in my direction. He lit his with a steelcase lighter but motioned for me to use the book of matches in front of me on the coffee table. I thought about firing the whole book and throwing it in Vin's face for a minute. For a minute.

"We were in the army together, Smitt, you and me." He puffed the smoke in and out dreamily. But his eyes were hungry in their hollow sockets.

"I hardly knew you, Vin. You were my superior officer."

"We spoke a few times. I liked you. That's why I remembered you."

"I was a lousy soldier."

"You weren't bad."

"I stunk. I drew flies, I stunk so bad as a soldier. I hated it and didn't give a damn about anything but my own ass. And I was scared as hell most of the time. All the time."

"You're a modest man, Smitt." Half his face smiled.

"Everybody was scared."

"Not the way I was."

"You went home with an honorable discharge."

"That's a laugh. I went apeshit when I got that letter saying Karen was married. I went off my nut and went out and slept with every slant-eyed thing with two legs that came along. You know how I got that discharge? Discharge is right. I got it for the eight kinds of VD I caught over there."

"Don't make me sick, Smitt."

"I'm making myself sick. If I'd been an enlisted man they'd've tossed my in the brig instead of home. Shit. I don't exactly feel like taking a stroll down that memory lane. So why not let it alone, Vin. Okay?"

"Shut-up, Smitt."

So now "war buddy" Vin turns nasty, huh? "Okay, pal, it's your gun."

"I said shut-up, Smitt."

I did.

"Your full name is Phillip James Smith, you are a veteran of the Korean War, presently working as a freelance insurance investigator."

He looked at me as if he expected an answer; since he hadn't asked a question I didn't have one for him.

"Well?" he asked. Demanded.

"Well what?"

"Is what I've said correct?"

"Yeah, yeah, so what?"

"And you carry a firearm?"

"No."

"You don't? Don't try lying to me, Smitty."

"I own a gun, but I've never carried it with me. It's a little .32 revolver. I never even fired it once. Carried it on a couple jobs, few years ago, but that's about it."

"Go get it."

"What?"

"The gun. Your gun. Go get it. But no shells, please. I've got shells for you. Then throw on some clothes and we'll get moving. Hustle, Smitt."

"What's going on?"

He showed me a plastic I.D. of some kind which identified him as an FBI agent. Looked legit, as far as I could tell.

"So," I said, "Uncle Sam wants me."

"You might say that."

"Well he can't have me. He had me once and that was one time too many."

"I'm got giving you a choice, Smitt."

"I have to take the gun?"

"Yes."

"But it's just a .32, wouldn't stop a fly..."

"If you have to shoot, aim at the head."

"If I have to shoot...what kind of shit is this...?"

"Hurry up."

The man driving the car kept his mouth shut the whole time. He wore a black suit which looked slept-in and a black tie which was food-stained and black shoes which looked like they'd just finished kicking somebody's teeth in. I noticed all of that because I was practically sitting on top of him; Thompson, the driver and I were all piled into the front seat of a black Lincoln Continental. There was a solid partition, a black padded wall without a window or anything, separating the front from the back. So I didn't know who or what the hell was back there. Nor by this time did I care. Still had the migraine, paisley spots floating in front of my eyes.

The heater was on heavy and it was hot in the car, as crammed together as we all were, though outside it was cold, crisp October. The driver switched off the heater and rolled down the window. Since I was sweating like a pig on a barbecue, I took this as a gesture of good will.

"I appreciate that, buddy, thanks a lot." I gave him a cheerful look.

The driver cleared his throat and shot a clot of mucous out the window. Then he rolled it back up and let me sweat some more. He turned his head toward me for a moment and his face looked like a slab of cement with a single crack running across it. An unfriendly crack at that, surrounded by pockmarks.

I didn't speak to him again.

"I don't have to tell you I don't like any of this, do I?" I asked Thompson.

"I didn't exactly expect you to, Smitt."

"How do I know this is on the level, really FBI and all?"

"You don't."

"How do you know I'll even go though with the damn thing, whatever it is?"

"You will carry it out, just as I outline it to you, because if you don't you'll sour my entire assignment and I'll be forced to eliminate you."

"Just like that."

"Just like that."

"You motherfucker."

"Shut-up, Smitty."

I did.

We drove on through the cold crisp October night and I pretended I didn't hear the sounds going on behind the black padded partition. Unidentifiable sounds, but sounds. Then I relaxed. Tried to ignore the press of Vin's automatic in my side.

The whole damn set-up sounded far-fetched as hell, but then I didn't have much say about it.

Vin and his men were assigned to guard the daughter of Edward Stewart, a United States Senator who'd been murdered a few weeks before. The daughter, whose name was Susan - Suzie to her friends - had seen the murderer, but hadn't revealed her knowledge until recently, within the last several days. I'd seen the girl's picture in the papers; it had been getting some big press. I asked Vin why she'd waited to talk and he told me that she was twenty years old and probably scared half out of her mind, which I could easily understand. After all, I was thirty-five and completely scared out of my mind.

Anyway, Vin and a couple other government agents were supposed to watch Susan Stewart closely, until proper steps were taken. Whatever the hell the proper steps were.

Now and then I would stop and ask Vin a clarifying question or two and Vin would tell me to shut-up. But I was pretty well convinced of all this. As you would've been, had someone with an automatic been doing the convincing.

The pay-off was that there'd been some related emergency come up in the past few hours which called for Vin and all of his men. And they needed someone to watch the girl for the hour they'd have to be gone, the exact hour being three-thirty to four-thirty a.m. Fifteen minutes away. And I was the lucky candidate. Why me, you ask? Don't you think maybe I was asking that question enough?

Not that Vin didn't have some answers for me. He and I had been friendly during Korea and he knew I lived in the city, since we'd exchanged goddamn Christmas cards for a few years after service. And, because I was an insurance investigator, I was in some vague way further qualified for the job. According to

Vin he immediately thought of me when he'd gotten in this spot, and supposedly the "office" Vin worked out of had prepared a list of likely civilians to recruit in such emergencies. And I was the only one on this sucker list Vin knew personally.

So there I sat. In the front seat of a black Lincoln Continental, a manned automatic sitting on my one side and a hunk of pock-marked concrete on the other.

At five till four the driver brought the Lincoln to a halt in front of an aging brownstone.

It had to be said, and the nerve to say it came to me, God knows from where. "Damn it, Vin, what is all this crap you're spoon-feeding me supposed to mean? How can you expect me to believe you? That you can't spare just one of your men for this task? And how can you be sure I'll be an obedient dog and not just head for the proverbial hills after you guys dump me off?"

Vin shrugged, backed the automatic off. The long-lost-war-buddy look took over his face again, "I'm not going to wave any flags, Smitt, but..."

"Put a hold on that crap, pal. It won't take with me. You say for security sake you can't call the cops, so you haul in a civilian, take him into your confidence and lay the whole bag on his shoulders. My ass! And why me, for Christ's sake, Vin, I'm anything but a hero. Hell, man, you could've done better picking a bum off the..."

"You hold it, Smitt. I told you we couldn't tell you

everything. Do you want to know too much? It's on your shoulders, you say, and why you? I said this was spur of the moment, Smitty, I'm taking a chance, a big one. Believe me, my head'll be on the chopping block if you blow this. It isn't the way I want it, Smitty, but so help me God it's the only possible way it can be."

I sat there for a moment.

"Well, Smitt?"

"Give me a cigarette, damn it."

He did, lit it for me off the dash lighter.

"What would you do, Vin, if I got out of this car and walked away from it?"

Vin lifted his shoulders and set them back down. "Not a damn thing, Smitty. Not a damn thing."

I bit my lower lip. Sure, sure he says I can walk away. But those eyes, damn flint-gray deep-socketed eyes say he'll shoot me down as I get out of the car. Let me fall to the gutter as he drives off.

"I'll do it."

"Good, Smitty, good."

Play the Star-Spangled Banner, why don't you, you red-white-and-blue bastard? Damn you, damn, damn, damn this whole thing anyway. If security's so important, doesn't that mean I'll be a loose end left to tie up, to make sure the secret's still a secret? No, never - the FBI wouldn't do that. Like hell.

"I'll do it. Not that I really had a choice."

Vin shrugged again. He did that a lot. "Okay, Smitt, let's get out of the car and I'll introduce you to Suzie Stewart."

"That sounds like a new doll from Matel."

"Just get out and we'll get your babysitting over with. We're on a pretty tight time schedule, you know, Smitt. Oh. Here's a box of shells for you."

Some babysitter.

When I got out of the Lincoln I tried looking into the back seat to see who or what was behind the black panel, but the windows were shaded, like a hearse. Vin tugged me along and we went up the half flight of stairs. Behind us concrete-slab sat at the Lincoln's wheel, gunning it now and then. Sounded like a purring cat. Jungle cat.

Inside the brownstone, beyond the vestibule, were more stairs, four flights of which we climbed, ignoring dozens of closed numberless prison-gray doors on each different floor. The building was unnaturally soundless. Like a massive tomb. The smell of paint was in the air.

Finally, on the fourth floor around the corner and at the end of a narrow corridor, waited another of the unnumbered grey cells. Vin gripped the automatic firmly as he worked a key in the Yale lock. He eased the door open, whispered:

"Vin, Hal."

"Okay. He with you?"

"Yeah."

The room was dimly lit and sparsely furnished. It smelled musty, like a run-down funeral parlor. The color scheme of the room was in charming faded browns: two chairs, a bureau, a bed and a standing lamp wearing its shade crooked. There was a doorway to the left of the bed, either to a closet, I supposed, or to the john. Possibly the john, because there was no one in the room except Vin, his buddy Hal and me. And I didn't think Susan Stewart would be waiting in a closet.

Hal said, "You Smith?"

I said, "Me Jane."

Vin frowned, said, "Cut it out, Smitt."

"Sorry," I said to Hal, "just trying to brighten a dreary situation. Glad to meet you, Hal."

I held out my hand to Hal and got a sneer in return.

"Don't mind Hal, Smitty."

But I did. I did mind Hal, Hal's attitude, Hal's B.O., and Hal's neanderthal appearance. This was an FBI man? He wore a tacky brown suit two sizes too small for his five foot wide frame and white socks glared up over his brown shoes. All of him but the white socks blended in nicely with the room's mud-brown decor.

"Where's Miss Stewart?" I dropped a spent cigarette to the floor and ground it out.

Hal jerked a thumb toward the door by the bed. From behind the door came the sound of a flushing toilet, and I deduced that it concealed the john and not a closet and watched as it opened and Susan (a.k.a., Suzie) Stewart came out.

She wasn't bad. Not the Playmate of the Month, mind you, not top heavy enough for that. She reminded me so much of someone else it shook me.

But she wasn't Karen. She was just a nervous young thing with hands moving around as if looking for someone to latch onto and full lips twitching and her lean long-legged body shifting uneasily as she walked over to me.

"You...you're mister...mister Smith?"

"Yeah. Smitty'll do. Glad to know you, Miss Stewart," and she took my hand and shook it. She had a nice soft hand, smooth, but no fishy grip either. Who needed Hal?

"I'm going to have to lock the door, Smitty," Vin told me. "You won't have a key. In approximately an hour I'll be back and relieve you of Miss Stewart and that will be all."

"I turn in my badge so soon?"

"That's right, Smitt."

"Okay by me. What if somebody tries to get in?"

"Anyone who is supposed to get in will have a key."

"What about...unwanted guests?"

"Better use that box of shells I gave you and get that .32 of your loaded up."

"Now, come on, Vin, come on!"

"I'm leveling with you Smitt. Load it. And use it if you have to." Half-smiled. "Aim at the head, remember?"

"Yeah, I remember."

He motioned Hal out, patted me on the shoulder and give me his weird almost-smile and closed the door. I heard him working the lock on the other side. And that was it.

"Trapped," she said.

She smiled, gently. Pretty girl, shoulder length hair, darkish blonde, eyes big bright and brown, wisp of a nose, nice lips, teeth with a sexy little buck to them, clean clear complexion, pretty girl.

"How did you...get into this, Smitty?"

I shrugged, a habit I picked up from Vin. "I don't know, Miss Stewart. I don't know. But I sure am in it."

"You seem...seem different, somehow...than what they said...said you'd be."

"Thanks." As nervous as she was, I half thought they'd told her to expect the Boston Strangler.

"I...I didn't mean anything bad...just...just that they said..."

"What did they say?"

"Nothing...nothing at all."

"Tell me, kid. What have you got to lose?"

"I'm sorry...sorry...maybe I shouldn't be talking to you...maybe we better...it'd be better not to talk... they'll be mad."

Shrugged again. "I don't care, Miss Stewart. I'd rather talk to you, though. Might help me to piece some more of this together so I could understand it a little."

Her mouth took on a slightly pouty look; eyes teary. "It's better...better not to understand. Care if I...sleep a while?"

"Go ahead."

She reclined on the bed. The short dress hiked up

over long nyloned legs. Lovely legs.

I looked away.

I opened the box of shells and loaded the .32. It was coldly new, though ten years old. Unfired. I hadn't shot a gun since Korea, and then unwillingly. Damn. Started filling the cylinder of the little revolver with the bullets. Looked over at the girl, who had fallen asleep. Nice girl. Pretty. Looked a little bit like Karen. Quite a bit like Karen.

Karen.

Karen, that bitch.

Married in some suburb with a bunch of brats hanging on her and her bastard Brad with his fifty thou a year. Fuck 'em.

I got a Christmas card from them once, had their picture on it, Karen, the bastard, the brats and a Collie who looked like the bastard only more intelligent. The bastard. Lucky bastard.

Damn Christmas cards anyway, Christmas cards to Vin Thompson helped get me in this hole in the first place. And damn Karen for being Karen.

Susan Stewart, pretty like Karen, so much like Karen, or like Karen was. So pretty. But nervous, so nervous.

And why not? Of course she's nervous, her father dead and her the only witness. Her father was an important senator, too, by God what was it he was involved in? Hearings on organized crime, wasn't it? A lot of people could have wanted him dead, and the kind of people who wouldn't mind making him that way.

Not to mention some of the "straight" people involved with organized crime who sit at their fat corporate desks and tsk tsk the high crime rate. The kind of people who don't like to look at the truth themselves, let alone let others look at it. Maybe Senator Stewart was clearing some of the fog away and somebody didn't like that. A lot of people like fog.

And I was one of those people sitting in the fog and wondering just what the hell was going on.

The girl slept.

I laid the .32 on my lap and leaned back in the hard chair and stared at the door and at the girl and back again, shifting from one to the other every minute or so, girl, door, girl, door...

At four-fifteen my bladder beckoned and I headed for the can. It wasn't the cubby-hole I'd expected, but was large, with tub, sink, head and even a window. Beyond the window, a fire escape. Good thing to know. The window was locked already, to my relief.

Back to the chair.

Four-twenty.

Outside the door, noise. Footsteps. Careful footsteps, but plainly footsteps, coming down the corridor. I eased over to the bed, placed my hand over Susan Stewart's mouth and jostled her awake. Her eyes golf-balled and sounds tried to come out of her, but I wouldn't let them.

"Trouble, maybe," I whispered.

She began to tremble.

"Easy, Suzie, easy. Please. Stand over at the left of

the door. Over in the corner. Quick!"

She rose and padded quietly across the room and molded herself as well as she could into the corner. She was terrified. Almost as terrified as I was.

Key in the lock, moving in the lock, working in the lock.

Door exploded open.

Hal.

Hal stood in the doorway and fired an automatic and fired it and fired it, not aiming at anything, not bothering to look at anyone. He emptied the gun. Then he looked to see if he had hit anyone. Which he hadn't.

"Nobody's that stupid, Hal," I said, "except maybe you."

I lifted the .32 at him, quivering, my face as tight as a clenched fist, my vision a searing, brilliant red. Squeezed the trigger. The gun belched fire at him and I squeezed some more and it belched more fire at him.

And Hal stood there and grinned at me.

I couldn't be that bad a shot, good God no, not at six feet!

Yet there Hal stood, grinning, stuffing another clip of bullets into his automatic.

It was then that I realized that there wasn't anything wrong with my gun, and probably not even with my aim: only the bullets. The bullets I'd been given were blanks.

I noticed too that Suzie was screaming, screaming a strange sort of a scream. Soft, sort of, and to herself. Almost distant.

And Hal was bringing the automatic up toward me and saying, "Now get the hell over against that wall and wait."

He's not going to kill us yet, I thought. He'd been aiming after all, aiming to miss us. Just trying to scare hell out of us, I guessed. Which he had. But, Sweet Christ, he was not going to kill us yet! There was time, time!

Time, time if only I wasn't so God Almightily scared, my stomach such a queasy mass of jelly, but I had to keep my guts from flying apart somehow.

"Hand over the .32, Smith," Hal told me. Softly, as to a child.

I just looked at him.

"I want that .32 , Smith."

I managed, "Go fuck yourself, Hal."

Hal showed me his teeth, two rows of hard yellow pencil erasers. He backhanded me. Blood crawled down my chin from a half-mashed upper lip. I fought the tears but some rolled out anyway.

"Cry, you little chickenshit." Hal spat on the floor. "Now hand me the .32. I've got some slugs that'll work in it okay." He laughed down low in his throat. The laugh sounded like a foot stepping in mud. "You'll see how good that .32 works with live bullets."

In neon letters the word formed in my tiny brain: frame.

"The neighbors, Hal," I heard myself saying. "What about the neighbors?"

Suzie, who'd stopped screaming sometime ago, said, "Do you seen any neighbors around to help us? He shot that gun off over and over again and do you see anybody?" Her voice sound flat, a mixture of shock and reconciled doom.

Hal said, "This place was done over, not long ago. Remodeled. Used to be an apartment house, then sat for years vacant. But they made it back into an apartment house, ain't it swell? Only nobody moves in till next week."

"This is a well-planned mess. You going to tell me about it or anything?"

"What's to tell?"

"Look, Hal, you're going to kill me in a while. Don't I have a right to know why? Humor Suzie and me, chum. Just a simple explanation."

He shook his head. "I don't give a damn why you die or what you know. And I ain't going to stand around beating my gums so you can die happy. Not that you'd understand any of it, anyway. Got it? Now hand me the .32 like a good boy and go over to the wall and stand with your hands behind your head. You, too, honey. Now move!"

We didn't move an inch.

"Look, chickenshit, hand me that .32 or I'll make things tough on you."

"You don't hear so good, Hal. I said go fuck yourself."

"Hand it over!"

I swallowed hard, grabbed in as much air as I

could, and heaved the .32 at his head. It caught him, and he pitched backward, the automatic firing into the ceiling. Bits of plaster and wood rained on me as I leapt at him. I had an idea of getting the automatic away from him, but mainly just wanted to kill him any way I could. Tried for his groin, couldn't get there, went after the throat, both hands, got there, dug in deep, tore at it, saw my hands go white, my nails red. Hand, his hand, came up at me with a gun in it, I batted it away with my elbow, lost grip on his throat. Got a good knee in his groin, finally, he screamed, high, but slammed in my nose with the gun barrel, didn't break it but blood gushed out, kept gushing. Automatic's single eye stared me in the face, in the eye, left eye, death staring at me. Gun went off, as I jerked my head to one side, sparks in my eye, burning, as gun went off to left of me. Punched my fist into his face, broke a knuckle, sent in a knee to his kidneys that drew him into a screaming ball. I grabbed up toward his arm, he had gotten to his feet now, grabbed his wrist and twisted it around.

The automatic went off and caught him square in the face.

I looked up and saw his face. What had been his face.

Watched as he dropped.

Suzie had started in screaming, only not so distant this time.

I went over to try and comfort her, but couldn't make it. Ran to the bathroom and puked. Puked till I puked blood.

Then wept.

I fell to the floor and buried my head in my hands and wept and coughed a racking cough and lay there in the puke and blood and tears and wished I'd let Hal kill me.

A few minutes passed and I began to snap out of it.

I struggled to my feet, bracing myself on the bowl of the head, and went over to the sink and washed up as well as I could. My upper lip throbbed and hurt and looked like yesterday's meat. I ached where I'd caught one in the kidneys and my nose was too sore to even think about. My knuckle was puffy-looking and numb, and my stomach felt weak from puking. And there was a taste in my mouth, an awful clinging terrible taste, a mouthful of pus and cotton.

But all in all I wasn't so bad off for what I'd been through. When I went back into the room I found Suzie staring at Hal's body. She'd covered his face with a pillowcase.

She said, "Somehow he doesn't seem...quite so very dead that way...you know?"

I didn't say anything. There's only one kind of dead, and that's dead, but I didn't say anything. I just picked up my .32 and went over to Hal's body to get the live ammunition for it. It was in his left inside sportscoat pocket. The pillowcase slipped and I had to see some of what was left of his face while I searched out the box of slugs, but my stomach seemed to hold on pretty well. Not that there was anything much left for it to retch up.

"Suzie," I said. Softly. Very.

"Yes?"

"You'll have to tell me about it. Everything."

"I know. They're going to kill us, aren't they?"

"Sooner or later."

"What'll we do?'

"Try and make it later."

"How?"

"Well, they'll be all over the neighborhood before long. Unless we stumble on a cruising cop first, we're had. I doubt we make it out of this section of the city alive, not at this hour, with them after us. The streets'll be deserted and we'll be like the proverbial..."

"The proverbial sitting ducks," she said. And smiled.

And smiled, for God's sake.

So did I.

"How about a public phone, there's surely one around here someplace, Smitty,"

"No go, kid. Bars are long since closed, and as for a booth, we can't stand around in one spot that long. If we could find one. No, we'll have to find some place to hide till the streets get busy. Toward mid-morning, when the people are thick on the street, we can blend into the crowd and then maybe get away because it'd attract too much attention if they shot at us in broad daylight."

"What will we do, Smitty, what can we do?"

I latched onto her hand. I pulled her in close and looked her right in her pretty Karen face and said, "You are on my side, aren't you, kid? I killed a man tonight and if you're not on my side I'm liable to do other things."

Her thin arms wrapped around me and she held herself close to me, warm to me, soft to me, saying, "I'm on your side, Smitty. On your side all the way."

I put my hands on her waist and held her away from me. "Then come on. Let's get the hell out. In the john, out the window."

"Huh?"

"Fire escape, kid, follow me."

"All the way, Smitty."

The scape got stuck toward the bottom and I had to jump half a story. Suzie eased down into my arms and I set her down and we stood and brushed ourselves off, looking all about us. No sign of anyone. I kept the .32 tight in my shaking hand, moving it in front of me back and forth in a steady swinging arc, a pendulum extending from my shoulder.

"You...scared, Smitty?"

"Shitless."

She laughed. "So am I. Boy, so am I."

I smiled at her. Going to get killed any minute and she's laughing. Well, what the hell, and why not? Hadn't I smiled back?

I turned and looked down the alley. A block down, a solid block down uninterrupted by streets, two tight walls of building on each side, the alley stopped in a dead end. The dead end was the back of an old factory of some kind: faded lettering read "Christie Brothers Manufacturing Company." I could see steps presumably leading down to a back entrance.

"Come on, Suzie," I whispered.

And we ran, footsteps echoing.

The door had an old-fashioned key-hole lock, and all it took was a good swift kick to pop it open and in we went.

It was a dusty dump, but it was home.

There were a couple dozen old wooden crates of various sizes scattered about the room. Which wasn't very big, as rooms go: long and narrow and naked, a boxcar of a room. The floor held a good inch of dust and the cobwebs hung from the low ceiling like old lace curtains.

The first thing we did was barricade the door behind us with three of the sturdiest crates. Another door, opposite the one we'd just entered by and leading, most likely, into some part of the deserted old factory, we likewise barricaded with two heavy boxes. There were several windows, but they were smoked with age, so there was no sweat to that. I cleared a spot in one corner and dusted off two crates for us to sit on and piled all the others in front of us.

I sat down on one of the crates and she sat next to me and we smoked two of the ten cigarettes I had left. The burning tips glowed in the room like lights on a boat lost in fog.

"I like you, Smitty," she whispered. All the rest of the time we talked it was in whispers.

"I like you too, Miss Stewart."

"That...that isn't really my name."

"The hell..."

"I'm not Suzie Stewart."

Shrugged. "I was kind of afraid of that. It was a sucker play, wasn't it."

"I don't know what it was, Smitty."

"Who hired you? Vin?"

"Mr. Thompson, you mean?"

"Yeah, him. Was it him?"

"Yes."

"It's coming slow, but it's coming."

"Smitty?"

"What?"

"Who do you work for?"

"Who do I work for? Well, starting alphabetically, I guess it'd be Ace Insurance, Acme Insurance, Atlas Insurance, Carolina Casualty..."

"No...I mean really. Really."

"Really. Ace Insurance, Acme Insur..."

"I don't get it, then, Smitty."

"Look, Suzie, we'll have to piece it together bit by weary bit, okay?"

"Okay."

"First off, who the hell are you?"

"I'm Susan Wynn, a secretary."

"Well, that's something at least. I can still call

you Suzie."

She smiled a nice little smile. Nice even in the dust and dark. "Does it matter to you?" she asked, and I said it didn't.

"Are you going to kiss me, Smitty?"

"Yes, and lots of other things as soon as we get this figured out."

"Kiss me now, Smitty. We may not get it figured out at all."

She was right, so I kissed her and it was fine. The dust and the cobwebs and the blood of somebody dead on my hands and all of it didn't matter. It was fine.

"I hope I get to kiss you a lot more, Suzie. A million times more. I hope sometime next week you and I will be kissing each other in the hot sun on warm white sand somewhere. And since I'd like to be doing that with you next week somewhere, alive, I'm not going to kiss you for a while so we can figure this out and try to save our skins."

But it was too late. She had started to cry and I had to kiss her again, soft and warm and with her tongue touching my teeth lightly and the salty taste of her tears, and then I was touching a white, rose-tipped breast, then kissing it, and her soft young body was all around me on the dusty floor and it was too late. Karen, I thought once, but only once.

"Will we be killed?"

"Shush. I'm thinking."

She held tight to my waist and we lay huddled together in the dirty corner, behind the crates.

"Let's go over it again, slowly," I said, ignoring the dry coat of grime on my lips.

"All right, Smitty."

"Thompson came to you as a representative of the government and asked your help. Very spur of the moment, as it was with me."

"Yes...but how spur of the moment was it, really?"

"Not very. Obviously they've groomed us for our roles for quite some time. I was chosen because Vin knew me and knew I wasn't the biggest hero the world had ever seen, knew I'd probably panic and blow sky high when thrown into a situation like this. And because he thought I could be easily browbeaten into it in the first place. My being a coward was his ace in the hole."

"You're no coward."

"How many heroes do you know of run into the can and puke their guts out?"

"Life isn't a movie, Smitty."

"You call this living?"

"But Smitty, why'd they pick me for this?"

"You have a superficial resemblance to the real Susan Stewart. Who has a superficial resemblance to a girl named Karen, to whom I was almost married. Once. A long time ago."

"Another reason why you were chosen for a leading role?"

"Right. And another reason why you were chosen for yours. You, too, have a superficial resemblance to Karen. Psychological warfare. Your resemblance to my Karen is the mental torture chamber those bastards have planned my breaking point around."

"I'm following this...I guess. But what's it all about?"

"Organized crime or someone involved with it trying to keep Senator Stewart's death a mystery, I assume. Vin and his pals are either in it themselves, or hired by someone who is. Being involved in the murder of said senator makes it follow that they're wanting to kill Susan Stewart, the only witness. I was supposed to be framed for it."

"How?"

"Well, I was set in that room guarding you with a gun loaded with blanks. I suppose that set-up was meant to get me to fire that gun and plaster my hand with power burns and such, which, incidentally, I did. Then my gun, with live ammunition, would be used to kill the real Suzie Stewart - who was probably being held captive in the backseat of the Lincoln they brought me over in - and I'd be set up as the murderer."

"On what motive?"

"Some Mob plant would point out Susan Stewart's resemblance to Karen, and of my mental hang-up about Karen, supported by some stunts I pulled in the service following my getting jilted. And it would be assumed by all that I'd simple wigged out, killed Miss Stewart in the process of losing my marbles over her resemblance to an old love of mine."

"Do you really think they could make that stick in a courtroom?"

"Hell no. They'd have to kill me and make it look like I shot the Stewart girl and then committed suicide or something. No, Hal wasn't about to let me leave that room alive. Vin was used to lure me there; some time was allowed for Vin to get well away; and then Hal came back to do his number."

"What about me?"

"They probably set it up so that various people in the neighborhood saw you going into that building earlier, of your own free will - and then the late Miss Stewart would be substituted for you in the dead of night. I guess. Otherwise I don't really know why they chose to drag somebody else in who they'd just have to get rid of later, but they obviously did. Lives don't mean a hell of a lot to them and to those guys you and me are just two more expendables."

She gripped me tighter and quietly wept into my chest until she fell asleep. I sat and smoked and stroked her hair now and then and kept my shaking hand with the gun in it leveled at the center point between the barricaded doors.

I smoked down to two cigarettes.

I waited.

I tried praying for a while.

Dawn wasn't far off, not more than half an hour.

Suzie woke up and we had the last cigarettes and talked for a while and kissed and made love again and talked for a while longer.

We talked on and on, and she asked what would

happen if she got pregnant, and told her it was about the least of our worries at the moment. I got to know her pretty well, don't really have time to tell you all about her; there are things you'll just never be able to know, because you never got to meet her.

She was still holding on to me, tight, when the voices came.

"Hold your fire - police. All is under control. Hold your fire."

I breathed a sigh of relief.

But then how the hell was I to know for sure?

Well, I didn't care. I just didn't care. I'd hold my fire for a moment while I saw if it was really the cops or not, what the hell could that hurt.

They came in and I held my fire.

It was Vin and two others and Vin fired an automatic and a tongue of flame came out of the end of it and settled in Suzie's right breast.

She didn't have time to say anything before she died.

I saw Vin coming at me starting to say something and I remembered what he'd told me and I raised the .32 and aimed.

The bullet went in his forehead and he died much too quickly.

They have left me in this room, unguarded and untied. They figure me too much a coward to make a break for it or try suicide. Or maybe just too unimaginative to kill myself with a bunch of wooden crates. And they think it's amusing to make me share the room with the corpse of a woman whom I might have loved.

Dawn came, went.

They haven't caught me writing on this notepad with this felt-tip yet, unless they know and think it'll keep me out of trouble. I've been writing for hours now and it must be mid-morning. I have to write small but I have to write. I have to get it all said so I can leave it here where someone might find it and go after the men who've done these things.

One of them came in a while ago, one I hadn't seen before, and asked me some things; in the process, he explained some of it. Most of it came out like Suzie and I had figured, but some of the details would never be revealed to me. Some of it had died with Vin.

I still don't know for sure who these bastards are, but it's safe to say they're with the Mob or something. Hard to tell. Writing so small like this in the dark and all gets my head going off in different directions.

I have to write all the time and not stop much because when I do I look over at Suzie. And she's dead.

A couple of them came in and were arguing about what exactly to do with me. One just wanted me dead, another was still trying to figure a way to use me to cement the cracks Suzie and I made in their plans. I get the feeling we really fouled up things up for them. That's some reward, I guess, but damn little.

I wonder if the real Suzie Stewart is dead or alive?

Not that it really matters. None of it really matters, does it? Not now.

Karen? Is that you, Karen?

No?

Suzie? Suzie.

Hell, I like you better, anyway, Suzie.

They're coming now, Suzie, I hear them in that other room, the one beyond this one, I hear them, Suzie and they're--

A Look At: Murder—His & Hers: Stories

Nine enthralling short crime and mystery fiction stories from talented husband-and-wife duo Max Allan Collins and Barbara Collins.

This entertaining collection ranges from a late-night craving which drives a pregnant private eye out to a convenience store and into a hostage situation to a womanizing senator who tries to replace his dead mistress with a lookalike and a cat with an accusing gaze.

Each tale features the twist ending that fans will relish, while also being a little old-fashioned.

"Boasts a plot twist that Hitchcock or even Rod Serling fans will savor. Recommend this highly to all fans of mystery short fiction." – Booklist

AVAILABLE NOW

About the Author

Max Allan Collins was named a Grand Master in 2017 by the Mystery Writers of America. He is a three-time winner of the Private Eye Writers of America "Shamus" award, receiving the PWA "Eye" for Life Achievement (2006) and their "Hammer" award for making a major contribution to the private eye genre with the Nathan Heller saga (2012).

His innovative Quarry novels were adapted as a 2016 TV series by Cinemax. His other suspense series include Eliot Ness, Krista Larson, Reeder and Rogers, and the "Disaster" novels. He has completed twelve "Mike Hammer" novels begun by the late Mickey Spillane; his audio novel, Mike Hammer: The Little Death with Stacy Keach, won a 2011 Audie.

For five years, he was sole licensing writer for TV's CSI: Crime Scene Investigation (and its spin-offs), writing best-selling novels, graphic novels, and video games. His tie-in books have appeared on the USA TODAY and New York Times bestseller lists, including Saving Private Ryan, Air Force One, and American Gangster.

Collins has written and directed four features and two documentaries, including the Lifetime movie "Mommy" (1996) and "Mike Hammer's Mickey Spillane" (1998); he scripted "The Expert," a 1995 HBO World Premiere and "The Last Lullaby" (2009) from his novel The Last Quarry. His Edgar-nominated play "Eliot Ness: An Untouchable Life" (2004) became a PBS special, and he has co-authored two non-fiction books on Ness, Scarface and the Untouchable (2018) and Eliot Ness and the Mad Butcher (2020).

www.ingramcontent.com/pod-product-compliance
Lightning Source LLC
Chambersburg PA
CBHW011455170626
46814CB00009B/3059